THE TESLA EXPERIMENT

ORDER OF THE BLACK SUN - BOOK 10

PRESTON WILLIAM CHILD

Edited by
ANNA DRAGO

HEIKEN MARKETING

Operation Hydra

The Genesis Project

The Alcázar Code

The Louisiana Files

Bones in the Bayou

Mystery of the Swamp

Louisiana Blues

PROLOGUE

*C*eleste felt her stomach churn as she pulled the rope toward her, slowly. They could never detect her movement or she would be done for. Her small hands nervously reeled in the thick roughness of the rope while the group of shouting men passed the inferno from which she had just escaped. Her goat bleated in panic as she tugged on its restraint, but the men did not hear it over the din of the burning barn. What if they saw it? They would certainly follow the fibrous cord and discover her!

Her blue eyes stretched open in anxious observation as she took note of the detail before her, holding her breath. Their uniforms looked like the dirt of the ash fields and their black rider boots reached up to their knees over the thick fabric. On their collars and arms, in red and black, different symbols bent into words she did not manage to read.

Oh, Celeste could read just fine, but not these writings. They spoke some language the symbols she knew could not be employed in. There were cloned lightning sigils that could have passed as 's' in her alphabet, but on their arms the men wore a terrible symbol inside a black circle. She had no idea what it said, but she knew very well what it represented – DEATH.

1

Every time she saw this symbol there was only fear and death in its trail. Every time it appeared there would be much praying amongst her people and now she knew why. From under the massive horse cart where she was hiding Celeste watched her village burn, the people she knew now dead, their prayers silenced. Above the black smoke ascended to the heavens as if the terrible men who marched through wanted to tarnish heaven with their evil.

Among them she noticed a tall, slender man. His eyes were light and his hair fair, but he did not engage in any of the cruelty. In fact, he looked as lost as she felt, wearing no uniform even though he was one of them. It struck Celeste as very peculiar that he seemed to find the atrocities unbearable, yet he did nothing to antagonize the uniformed men or help the villagers. Suddenly his eyes caught hers. Celeste gasped.

It felt as if her little heart was going to burst with fright when he locked onto her, yet he did not move. Her goat bleated and stumbled about for fear of the fire, but she paid him no mind now. The man she was staring at sank his hands into his pockets and pulled from them a notebook and a pencil. Celeste cringed as a pair of shiny boots stopped right above her head, raising up dust into her face.

She needed to sneeze, but she knew it would be the end of her if she did. Her dirty little hand pinched her nose. Her goat got away from her and rushed out into the gravel road, but Celeste allowed him his escape from her, rather than to be foolish and pursue. The man who stood in front of her obscured her view of the other man she had been looking at and she rolled over to her left to get a better look. But he was gone.

Celeste tucked her little body back, deeper under the cart and closer to the wall it was standing against to utilize the shadows. From there she studied her surroundings, looking for the fair haired man. The black boots turned just as the cart began to shake. Celeste's eyes filled with tears as the uniformed man started scuf-

2

fling with something on the cart she could not see. Terrified, she knew she could not whimper in her weeping, not a sound to escape her lest she ended up another body on the burning pile a few meters off.

In her nostrils the stench of burning bodies choked her and she fought not to vomit. Horror filled her as she watched them burn, people she had known since she was an infant. Their faces were twisted, their eyes sunken away in their cavities and their lips curled back in death, revealing their teeth aside protruding tongues. Father Bleux's skin was black, chafing against the blistered breasts of Madame Marie, Celeste's first grade teacher. The nine year old girl thanked God that her parents were already dead a year before this hideous happening struck their town, because they would never die as horribly as the villagers they knew so well.

The sun was setting, but it looked like night already. Everywhere over the department of Haute-Vienne an evil loomed and the sun was blacked out by the snaking smoke of iniquitous butchery. Celeste pinched her eyes shut until the furious shaking of the vessel over her ceased. A bubbling death rattle sounded above her head and she saw a strong rain of blood stain the shiny boots of the soldier who had blocked off her escape before. At once, the rest of him fell to the ground, limp and bloody. Celeste started at his glaring blue eyes as they pierced hers, but soon she realized that they saw nothing anymore. He was dead from the gaping wound in his throat and his blood was streaming over the arid ground towards her amidst the screams of women and children still trying to flee the burning church they were locked in. Machine gun fire smothered their cries instantly.

A little piece of paper feathered down from the top of the horse cart, there where Celeste could not see. It landed just to the inside of the shadow where she hid. Before the rivulet of blood met the paper, she scooped it up and read the scribbling on it.

'WAIT FOR NIGHT. Then hide in the pea bushes.
   Help will come'

THE YOUNG CELESTE WAS PERPLEXED, but grateful for the help. Although she was not certain if the note could be trusted, she did as it had dictated. It was a strange piece of paper, the true reason for her confusion. It looked like a ledger, perhaps a letter head of a doctor or a business. But it did not look like anything from 1944 at all. Even to her juvenile eyes it was clearly peculiar. Ripped and stained by soot, she discerned only some letters and numbers on what used to be a notebook heading.

UNIVERSITY OF EDIN...H
   In th..ks f.. contribution...esteem...
   Facul...2015

"2015?" she frowned.

   Celeste tucked the note inside her dress pocket and elected to believe that the numbers could not possibly belong to a date. Whatever it stood for, her savior was associated with it and she vowed to remember him forever, even if she did not survive World War II.

CHAPTER 1

*P*urdue travelled for two days to see his friend from the old days in Birmingham before they parted at age twenty three and twenty six, respectively, to pursue different fields in physics and attended different universities. The billionaire inventor felt like going old school and bought a ticket for the train to take him to Lyon by invitation of Professor Lydia Jenner - old friend, once colleague and now terminal patient, bedridden in her final days of cancer.

She was three years Purdue's senior and the thought of her in the throes of terminal illness saddened him deeply. They had been friends for decades and now, in the prime of her life, barely forty seven years in age, she was dying. It felt strange for Dave Purdue to know that someone of his era, his age group, was now reduced to a frail and quivering victim where he felt as if his body still retained the qualities of a seventeen year old.

On the 22.27pm Eurotrack train from Paris he slept most of the time. He stayed reclusively in his own compartment that he paid double the fee for, just to be assured of no disturbance, save for the delivery of his dinner and breakfast by special staff. Not that he did not enjoy long trips. As a matter of fact, he deliberately elected to take the regional train to enjoy the trip which was about 4 hours longer than the fast train at his leisure. But he was exhausted from his flight from Edinburgh after two sleepless nights of reading and experimenting to create an electromagnetic device strong enough to upset inter-dimensional veils to the point of what Purdue dubbed *ripples.*

It was from this very experimentation that he was compelled to contact Lydia to obtain some advice in the field she had long ago conquered so successfully that she had been ridiculed as a madwoman and a reckless academic. In this regard she much reminded him of Dr. Nina Gould, strung up and hung high for being too passionate to control, but it seemed that Purdue was most attracted to women like this above all others. From the call he placed for her advice, he learned of her current condition which subsequently urged him to rather to visit the woman the academic world of Particle Physics and Quantum Sciences called a 'loose cannon.' Perhaps that was the case because he was himself a wild card in his academic circles. Only his fortune was his, well, fortune.

Had he not been independently wealthy he was certain that he would never have been afforded the amount of misdemeanor that he was, and most definitely he would not be called 'eccentric' for it. No, had Purdue been a man of average means he may well have been called insane for his ruthless pursuit of questionable theories to such an extent. It aided him well in his discoveries of the rules of the mysterious, but such knowledge as which he had attained also bordered on the freakishly dangerous.

A dreamless sleep overcame him just a few miles past the boundaries of Paris as the train travelled south toward Lyon, a trip that would last a few lazy hours for passengers to catch a breather from the day before arriving at their destination in the dead of night. Purdue had jokingly pondered upon the nature of people who chose this train as being coy breeds of vampires, maybe secret lovers, assassins or agoraphobic poets looking for an outing. The tracks were smooth under his train car, lulling him into a deeper sleep where the drizzle of the night wept against his tightly shut window.

In the corridor outside it was silent as most of the passengers were too tired to scuttle, apart from the occasional pee break or visit to the bar for a drink. Such peace was unusual in Dave Purdue's life. There was almost a feeling of apprehension attached to it, as if he knew in his subconscious that there would be a penalty for the serenity. Perhaps this was a product of his lifestyle of the past few years, the danger associated with his affiliations and the constant recurrence of prophecies locked in antiquities he could not resist investigating.

On the good side of his mind sat Nina Gould, the woman he had loved since the day he met her, regardless of her dismissal of him from the get-go. He had briefly managed to win her over, had the pleasure of her carnal affection and her company until this all too familiar association with arcane societies forced him to abandon her and his life as he knew it for a while. And when he had returned, found her attentions turned away from him, directed toward the only man who truly challenged him for Nina's heart – Sam Cleave, Pulitzer prize winning investigative journalist and, as Purdue now reluctantly admitted, friend.

Though the memories Dave Purdue's mind wandered, probing at long closed doors of terrible things to sate his masochistic appetite for moral punishment. His nightmares threatened just on the other side of those doors, the red light of hell falling in thin streaks on the floor from under them.

In those instances he would hear his twin sister's voice calling his name, speaking of his despicable betrayal not once, but twice in her life. When she would dissipate he would be lured to other doors where evil men he once treated like brothers would lurk, grinding their teeth and slamming their fists.

But Purdue would leave them all behind. Now he only looked forward, hastening towards the doors of knowledge and tranquility. He was done with the modern day Nazi's and their relentless search for occult satisfaction and material gain. Corny as it was to him, he would keep his eye only on Nina, the feisty and petite historian who had unfortunately been at the receiving end of his reckless nature far too many times. This was why he elected to steer clear of her and Sam for a bit. In fact, he did not even care if his absence promoted their love for one another anymore, as long as she did not hate him anymore for endangering her. Purdue's mind slid through this corridor within seconds and on the other side of the dark end there was a remarkable oblivion. No regrets, no nightmares pushing through and no guilt. He just slept.

At 2am a reluctant knock rapped at his door.

"Monsieur Purdue?" a lady's voice whisper-asked.

"Oui?" he mumbled from the dusk of his slumber.

"Your sandwich and tea, as you requested, Monsieur Purdue," she answered from the other side of the door. He shot a glance at the window. It was still thick night outside and the rain kept the glass wet.

"Merci," Purdue said as he took the tray from her trolley. The small, young woman looked mousy and sweet, but her expression was indifferent.

"Would you like me to alert you before we reach Lyon?" she asked.

"No. No, thank you, I'll be awake from now on," he smiled and closed the door with a click. He listened for her fading footsteps before he sat down to nibble on the Italian bread and cottage cheese she delivered with his Earl Grey. For some reason Purdue felt anxious about the rest of the train trip, but he could not find any reason to substantiate his suspicion.

He looked forward to see Lydia, but he did not want to imagine what the illness had done to her physically. It was something he would have to face, but he was not a man who knew what to say in such awkward and painful situations. Lydia was always a crazy, mischievous woman who felt that nothing was impossible. Nothing at all. According to her personal point of view, physics and geometry were the keys to just about every secret the world found impossible.

'Remember, David,' he recalled her words, *'just because we have not yet discovered the properties of the impossible, does not mean the impossible cannot be conquered. Mankind is a spec of nothing in the eyes of Creation and if science, as we know it, cannot explain something we deem it irrational.'* Purdue smiled, reciting her doctrine in his head as he had always done when he doubted his pursuits. *'Don't be fooled, old cock. Other dimensions run on other scientific properties, that's all. As soon as we acquaint ourselves with the unknown sciences, we will function like those beings we now dismiss as figments of madness. We will become the impossible.'*

"I hope you fight that final threshold until I have spoken to you, Lydia," he said softly, enjoying his light meal in the solitude he so needed. "Don't you dare die until I have seen you."

He checked his tablet for messages. There was one from Nina, dated the day before.

Hey Dave

I am guest lecturing in Lisbon and it is stunning where they put me up. I'll send some pictures later on. Met some bloke who is a technical genius and he wanted to exchange ideas with you regarding your laser research, so I thought to give you his number.

Don't know what you are up to, but I hope you are staying out of trouble, for once. I'll be home in Oban by month end, if you want to say hello. Let me know if you hear from Sam, alright?

Cheerio

Nina

PURDUE SMILED. It was good to hear from the beautiful historian again. Normally he had to establish contact first, so he felt flattered that she wrote out of the blue, with an invitation to her house, no less.

"So, Sam is not with you after all," Purdue said as he saved the message and took down the number she had included. He did not want to admit that he was relieved, but knowing that she was not with Sam cheered him quite a bit more than he cared to permit. After Dave Purdue answered his other e-mails and texts, he sipped the last of his tea and checked his watch.

It was June 9th, 2015, 00.35am.

He yawned, stretched and packed up the loose belongings he had unpacked before he fell asleep – a text book, a pocket watch and his can of deodorant. The train slowed down just as his alarm alerted him that they would reach Lyon in the next few minutes. When he emerged from his compartment he saw the trolley girl at the end of the passage, staring out into the darkness. There were no other passengers in his car as far as he could ascertain. Every partition he passed was neat and vacant, even though the train had barely come to a halt.

"Thank you for the lovely meal," he told the trolley lady.

He face was pale and void of emotion as she slowly turned to face him. She forced a smile, but all he could perceive was a terrible twist of doom in her.

"You are very welcome, Monsieur Purdue. Be safe out there. Goodbye," she replied blandly. Purdue stepped off the train, onto Lyon station's platform in the small hours of June 9th and looked back at the train that started to move on again.

From what his tired eyes reported, there was no-one in his car.

CHAPTER 2

*P*urdue checked into the Hotel le Royal Lyon just before 3am and found it hard to fall asleep again. More than the strange train car experience, he felt too excited to see Lydia and wished he had one of Nina's sleeping pills in his bag now. In this purgatory he remained, partaking in a plethora of baby bottles of liqueurs and brandy he discovered were included in his room fee. Delighted for the inebriation and ultimately, some sleep it would bring, Purdue enjoyed the pleasant old age atmosphere of the guest house and it's remarkably mild temperature, considering the season. It was hardly Scotland or Germany.

He set the television to National Geographic and finally succumbed to the gentle narration of the documentary, along with the soothing anesthesia of the alcohol.

In the morning he woke to the loud lock bolt next door. It was not too harsh, but it was far too early for him to rise and he turned to sleep on, unsuccessfully. Purdue sighed. His mouth was extremely dry and his head felt like a bomb testing chamber. The sleep would not come back, so he finally dragged himself out of bed to take a hot shower. Save for the headache, the shower did him a world of good. His skin felt refreshed and warm and he even enjoyed shaving, something he usually dreaded in the morning.

The Scottish billionaire had two bags with him on his latest travel venture – one valise with two changes of clothing and some toiletries and an unassuming brown leather case which contained a remarkable amount of technology that he reckoned he could perhaps run by Lydia. She was an expert in most subjects similar to those he dabbled with. Therefore, if she was not too perturbed by her malady, he hoped to pick her brain with some advice, shortcuts or suggestions as it were.

Purdue hired a car and driver familiar with Lyon and at 11am he left for Lydia's home in Brotteaux, an affluent neighborhood by reputation situated between the railway and the Rhône River.

"Course Franklin Roosevelt? And then toward the river, Monsieur?" the driver, Pascal, asked Purdue. Purdue nodded, and passed the small note he had scribbled Lydia's directions on to the driver.

"It should hopefully make more sense to you than it did to me. I'm afraid she changed her mind several times, but such is the nature of her illness. Confusion and lapse of memory," Purdue explained awkwardly.

"She is ill with confusion?" Pascal asked sincerely.

"Brain cancer, Pascal," Purdue replied.

The driver shook his head in pity for the lady and uttered a nasal whine, "That is very sad, Monsieur Purdue. Poor Madame Jenner. Your friend? Or family?"

The Audi S6 pulled away and glided along the rue towards the larger main road along the river where the barges lazily bobbed on the glint of the morning river ripples.

"Old friend, but still the news was hard to take," Purdue

said as he looked out the window at the deep blue of the Rhône. "Could you figure out her address from all those details?"

"Oui, Monsieur," Pascal nodded with a boastful smile. "I believe she lives in the chateau at the end of Rue Antoinette off this road. The house is known to stand alone, away from the other properties here that are mostly shops and museums and so on."

"Ah!" Purdue said, lightly tapping his hand on the car door where his forearm rested over the rolled down window. "A chateau?"

"Only by name, really," Pascal informed Purdue, casting quick looks in the rear view mirror as he spoke. "It is a manor, but not of remarkable size. Not by the standards of Versailles, at least!" He chuckled, joined by his passenger. Purdue knew what he meant about the palaces in France and how one could hardly call any regular mansion 'large' in comparison. "But it is known by most drivers in Lyon solely because it is so...out of place."

Purdue detected a bit of mystery in Pascal's tone, but he chose to let the matter be and spend the rest of the drive just pondering upon his visit. He wondered what poor state Lydia was in and if he was perhaps doing more harm than good by taxing her with his presence. But she was not the type to fold to mere burdens and Purdue hoped that she had still hopefully retained her adventurous personality.

While they stopped at a traffic light, Pascal switched on the radio for a bit of musical distraction, but it was time for the news. Purdue's French was alright, but it had been a while since he had heard it spoken in its native environment. A female voice with a professional and husky intonation reported on a fire that broke out in a laboratory in Geneva the night before and that over four hundred meters of the tunnel had been damaged, although not irreparably.

"Pascal?" he asked the driver as he pulled away again. "What tunnel is she speaking of? She spoke a bit fast for me to catch everything."

"Oh, uh, she said that a fire broke out in the tunnel of the CERN project in Geneva. Some of the machine was damaged but they can fix it," Pascal translated loosely in his easiest English.

"Oh my God!" Purdue replied, running his fingers through his hair and staring at the blue sky. "That is beyond dangerous! It could end the bloody world, you know."

Pascal shrugged and smiled faintly, "I don't know, I'm afraid. I am not much of a follower of science things. I know what CERN is, of course, but not how it works or what they really do there. I keep to sports. Football, Formula One and so, Monsieur."

Purdue nodded in acknowledgement, "I see. Yes, I don't mind a good bit of football myself."

But though he was chatting casually with his driver about sports, Purdue felt a spark of panic and curiosity flare up inside him as to the exact details of the incident. Eagerly his long fingers itched for his tablet, just to peruse the related articles until he reached Lydia's home, but he refrained. He was too close to his destination now to go hounding around on the Internet for accurate news.

"Here we are, Monsieur," Pascal announced.

He stopped at the tall gate and got out of the car, leaving the engine running. Through a thorny maze of branches that possessed the stone pillars where the gate was hinged Pascal buzzed the intercom and conversed briefly. Purdue could discern his own name and then the gate clicked and slid open. Being made of solid steel the gate did not allow Purdue a view of the mansion until it gradually slid aside, disappearing behind the sturdy stone wall that barely revealed itself from under the wild growth of foliage.

"There we go, Monsieur Purdue," Pascal groaned as he fell back into his seat and shut the door. "Shall I wait for you inside or will you call when you are ready to be collected again?"

Purdue thought quickly. It was a difficult decision. He was not sure how well she was to receive visitors. It would be awkward if he sent Pascal away and found that Lydia was mentally incapacitated or sedated. "Don't go too far," he smiled, amused at his own answer.

Pascal was a sharp tack. He caught on what his employer's predicament was and nodded politely, "I'll be right across the park at the restaurant, having some lunch. Ready to come when you summon, Monsieur Purdue."

"Good man," Purdue cheered with a pat on Pascal's shoulder.

But both men found the yard they drove through very peculiar. As the gate closed behind the Audi they became aware of an electrical charge along the inside of the perimeter wall. The place did not resemble at all the garden or terrace of such a posh mansion. Instead of plush brushes and elegant trees, flower beds and fountains there was only tall grass, gravel and overgrown, un-kept gardening. Rein-forced with what looked like steel plating, the entire fence wall ran nine foot high along the circumference of the yard. Rusty nails secured the plates crudely to the stone and mortar under the creepers and wild tree branches. The lawn was dry and brown, because, Purdue guessed, water would upset the charge he could hear vaguely between the plates.

It was very strange, but now he understood why the house had such a reputation of being singled out among the other properties. Even Pascal could tell something was amiss.

"I think I should rather wait here in the car, Monsieur Purdue," he remarked, gawking at the cracked and chipped statuettes all over the property. "If this is what the outside looks like there is no telling what you might find in the house."

Purdue gave it some thought.

"No," he cried finally, keeping to his light demeanor, "you go on, Pascal. Have some lunch. I'll be fine. Whatever is in that house, I can appreciate."

Pascal mumbled, "Oui, but can you outrun it?"

Purdue took his leather case and slung it over his shoulder, giving his driver a brief wave as he skipped carelessly up the cracked cement steps to the leave strewn terrace. A chair with a seat stained from months of mud and downpour rocked in the slight breeze at the far right side of the porch.

Purdue ignored the ominous looking surroundings and rang the doorbell. A stocky, abstemious creature opened the door. His eyes were weary, even in their coldness and his clothing painfully neat on every curve of his body. Purdue guessed the butler in his fifties, but his voice sounded ancient.

"Master Purdue," he said plainly, "welcome to Jenner Manor."

"You're British?" Purdue asked without thinking.

"Yes, sir. You expected a French maid?" the rigid man asked dryly.

Purdue had to laugh.

"Pardon me, friend. I meant nothing by it. I just did not expect…" he chuckled, but by the man's lack of enthusiasm for Purdue's humor, he swallowed his laughter. "Is Professor Jenner available? I know I am a tad early."

"That is not a problem, sir. Please, have a seat in the parlor and I will inform the professor of your arrival," the butler suggested and without sparing a moment for Purdue's response he disappeared up the stairs.

The inside of the house was not as dilapidated as the exterior, apart from the slightly wilted and dried up bouquets of flowers on the corner tables that gave the place an odd odor of old rot and stagnant water. But the tile floors were spotless, the walls lacking any art or photographs and left utterly bare throughout the hallway. Purdue stood in the dusty, faintly lit drawing room where the slightly separated drapes yielded to a tardy bit of sunray that accentuated the trickling dust particles settling in the room.

The furniture was completely out of place for the design of the classical manor. Purdue had to smile to himself at the sight of the plain couches and coffee tables of the sunken lounge floor that reminded him of a kitsch London apart-ment from the early seventies. The hearth was built in with bricks and instead of charming paintings adorning the walls as he would have expected, there was yet again nothing hung. Pastel green and cream sections of the walls revealed studded edges that he simply had to scrutinize.

Purdue frowned as his fingertips studied the short nails that ran from the ceiling to the floor where they had fixed yet another collection of sheeting to cover the interior of the room, perhaps all the rooms. He had to know why.

CHAPTER 3

*S*am woke up way too late. He had missed breakfast by hours and he had well a way to go before lunch would be served. And as he always had a solution for such little problems, he made for the mini fridge instead – to keep him occupied, as it were. The party from the night before turned out to be quite the anti-climax. Even though his intention was to gather information there, he ended up hoping for more and ended up being sorely disappointed. Her name was Lily and she would have been the perfect night cap, but she left with someone else before Sam could close the deal.

His cell phone shattered his hung over thoughts.

"Cleave," he grunted, wondering where his clothes were shed the night before as if the caller could see him.

"Sam Cleave! This is Penny Richards from the Cornwall Institute of the Sciences," a female voice chimed.

"Cornwall…in Ireland," Sam stated with distinct uncertainty.

"It's a surname, Mr. Cleave," she chuckled. "Bernard

Cornwall was the benefactor of our foundation, hence the name."

"Ah! I see," Sam replied, looking for his pants. "For a moment I thought I was caught in a science fiction novel, or perhaps a scientific experiment in the Bermuda Triangle."

He could tell the woman was smiling and did her best to be friendly, but her words were somewhat impatient. "Listen, Mr. Cleave, I was wondering if you have any new information on the imminent sabotage of the CERN LHC site."

She cleared her throat uncomfortably.

"I spoke to several people last night, Miss Richards," he reported, "but I'm afraid there was not much I could ascertain from the faculty. As I told your colleague Mr. Somanko yesterday, I don't think his ex-employee is involved in the sabotage. These threats came from someone more professional, a group of people rather than just one individual."

"So you are saying it is more serious than we thought?" she asked.

"Aye," Sam nodded. "I suggest you tighten up on security."

She paused for a moment, allowing Sam some time to locate his pants and open a tiny bottle of Southern Comfort for breakfast. He could hear her composing herself.

"Mr. Cleave, have you read the morning paper?" she asked in a much more serious tone. "Have you seen the morning news?"

"I have not," he admitted, although it was a terrible confession to make at this hour of the day.

She sighed hard, "A fire ravaged two kilometers of the CERN tube last night, Mr. Cleave. Were you sleeping on the job?"

"I'm sorry, I was ill during the night and only fell asleep at dawn, Miss Richards," he lied, swallowing the bourbon to get some hair of the dog. He felt ashamed for being so out of synch, so off kilter in his career. Of all people a Pulitzer winner, a renowned investigative journalist such as himself, should be on top of things. It was a shame that he was fraying at the ends like this to have lost his focus for but a night, yet neglected to know what the rest of the world already knew and looking utterly inept at his job.

"Look," she said more gently, "I understand that you do not need our support and that you are a celebrity journalist and author, but you accepted this assignment, Mr. Cleave, so please, I implore you to please show more enthusiasm for the case. If anything it would help us avoid another, perhaps bigger, catastrophe."

"You are correct, Penny. You are absolutely correct," Sam agreed sincerely. "I have been distracted and overslept this morning which does not reflect well on my reputation, but I assure you I will be following up on this incident."

"We will appreciate that, Mr. Cleave," she replied in clear relief. "Please make your way to tomorrow's conference in Geneva as soon as possible to see if you can shed some light on the arsonist in the meantime. I don't think it was any coincidence that some of our investment was destroyed within a week from the anonymous threat we received. God knows, I do hope it was just an accident, but we need to be sure."

"I shall leave this afternoon. Can you arrange a press pass or something similar for me at your convention? It is called the Cornwall...?" Sam asked, penning down the details.

"*Bernard Cornwall Trust.* That is the name you should look for at the Vidal Lux Hotel. I shall book a reservation for you there so long," she informed him.

"Got it. Thank you, Miss Richards," Sam said, relishing the warmth of the bourbon in his throat. He pressed the red button on his phone. "Jesus, could do with a fag now," he lamented, having run out of cigarettes just before he passed out on the bed a few hours before.

The whole thing with the CERN threats had him bothered. He was not hired by Penny's organization, but it was more like a mutual professional courtesy between them. The Cornwall Institute contacted Sam in hopes of him exposing an enemy of theirs that had been imperiling their projects for months. In return, should he find the culprit he would have exclusive rights to the story and yet again prove his worth in gold at exposing criminals to the world. It was a good deal for Sam. His book was still doing well, but he would not soon be donating sports stadiums to cities or buying yachts for random laid off fathers for charities. Now and then Sam Cleave still took on a worthy story to see if he could get to the bottom of the sewer of deception to retrieve what was left of fairness.

"Well, Sam, no time like the present," he sighed to himself as he headed for the shower. With heavy feet he sauntered into the overwhelming white plastic environment of the en suite bathroom. *Maggie's Bed & Breakfast* certainly knew how to make cheap look pretty, but he was not about to judge an establishment with such a good array of liquor stashed in their rooms.

AFTER CHECKING out just before 2pm, Sam made it just in time for his 3.40pm flight from Dublin to Heathrow. He hoped that no unforeseen obstacles like weather or mechanical problems would perturb his urgent trip to Geneva, but for now such concerns would not benefit him. What did vex Sam while he found himself in lonely moments on the plane, was that he had no idea exactly why someone would sabotage the CERN project, since it was not something substantial for the criminal world.

Next to him sat a gentleman who, to Sam's relief, was not a talker. However, he did look like a complete drip from an old horror film. Small, round spectacles rested on a long, crooked nose and his white grey hair stood on end as if he had poked his index finger at a power point. A small goatee extended from his chin, but it was horribly untidy and frizzled. Sam taxed his ocular muscles to look at the man without turning his head. As the image dictated, the man wore a bowtie with his cardigan and brown pants.

The old man caught Sam glaring, even in his meager glances.

"Hello," he said to Sam.

"Good afternoon," Sam smiled self-consciously.

"Anything interesting about me, then?" he asked the journalist outright.

Sam felt awful for being discovered in his curiosity. It was a first class flight, therefore he knew that the old man who spoke to him could not have been just any old fool. Quickly Sam paged through his mind's reserves for a proper explanation and, to his own surprise, he found a good one.

"My apologies for staring, sir. And I hope you don't take insult to this, but..." Sam hesitated, "...you remind me of a young Albert Einstein."

"Agh, vell!" the man exclaimed with a hearty grin. "Einstein is one of my idols. In fact, had it not been for his Unified Field Theory, I would not be sitting here next to you right now!"

"Really?" Sam smiled with relief.

"Yesh, yesh," the man replied gleefully in his heavy Dutch accent, "he was my inspiration to become a theoretical physicist."

"You are a theoretical physicist?" Sam gasped. He was truly surprised to have run into someone who happened to be in the same line of the people he was snooping for.

"Yesh, I am. Professor Martin Westdijk, University of

Utrecht Applied Physics," the old man smiled, extending a hand to Sam.

"Sam Cleave. Journalist, among other things," Sam replied, but he could not help but feel that he sounded extremely inadequate in title compared to the professor.

"Journalist? Interesting. Have you heard about the fire?" he asked Sam, as if he knew the Scotsman's business.

"Aye, this morning I…heard," Sam said.

"I tell you, those damn religious freaks always get in the way of scientific research. Why can't they just admit that science IS God and get a life, hey? Hey?" he shook his head, ordering a drink from the stewardess.

"Wait, what do you mean, Professor?" Sam asked, taking the same drink as his new friend.

"Well, CERN is constructing the super collider to mimic the Big Bang, so to speak, right? Now you have these fanatics going on about scientists 'playing God' and that we are going to cause the destruction of the planet if we create another Big Bang, destroying the world as we know it," he exclaimed, obviously caught in disbelief of the narrow mindedness of the people he referred to.

Sam shook his head. "I know. But they would be insane to set fire to something they already deem to be so unstable, right?" He had to fish a bit, even if it was just to obtain some background on the politics involved.

The old man grunted, chugged back his whiskey and looked at Sam though his small goggles with bloodshot eyes, "Correct! But then again, with what they know about the research we are trying to conduct, I would not be bloody surprised if they had no idea what could happen."

"Do they belong to an organization? Or is it just a group of people with similar beliefs?" Sam asked.

"I don't think so. Not the people who caused the fire," he

told Sam. Professor Westdijk leaned closer, "To be frank, I think the very people who worked on that section did it."

"But why would they?" Sam whispered. "All their work down the drain, or were they just working there because they infiltrated the project just to sabotage it?"

The old man waved off Sam's speculation with a frown and a shake of his head, "No, no, my boy. I can promise you they would not do all that just to destroy their own work. What I think is that it was two or three engineers or maybe electricians, sabotaging the working of the machine by just making a deliberate electrical mistake, hey?"

Sam gave it some thought. "Could very well be, but there must be more to it?"

"Look, from what I know in this life, I can tell you that sometimes you only need a force of morality, pressed on by fear, to do such drastic things. Whoever caused the fire caused the wires to short circuit and that takes skill, hey?" the old man argued.

"So you are saying that they just wanted to win time by setting back the construction and working of the machine?" Sam asked under his breath.

The old man tapped his hand with a crooked finger, "*That* is what I was thinking, Sam Cleave."

"Who would do that?" he wondered out loud.

"Other scientists," Prof. Westdijk answered.

"But why?" Sam asked him.

The old man shrugged, "Maybe they were busy with an experiment of their own. Maybe they were onto something bigger than just smashing particles together like a bloody toddler, hoping to see an effect."

Sam watched the old man's annoyance take form. He slowly peeked over the frame of his glasses. "Maybe they were upset that something as pointless as the LHC got funding while they were onto something so much bigger."

CHAPTER 4

*P*urdue's scrutiny was interrupted by the sound of murmuring coming from the main hallway. At the bottom of the stairs, a wheelchair crossed the landing with the stern butler chasing after it with much disgruntlement.

"Madam, please allow me to help," he insisted, but the woman in the chair would have none of it.

"Healy, I can do this. I'm not dead yet, you know!" she barked in a low, raspy voice that struck Purdue as some German actress from the heyday of cinema or some rock singer from Woodstock. Marlene Dietrich? Marianne Faithful? He smiled.

"Now get some wine as I asked you twenty bloody times already. Please," she grunted back at the poor butler as she wheeled herself into the drawing room.

"As feisty as ever, I see," Purdue smiled and approached her, but she waved him away cordially.

"Please, Dave, don't touch me. The chemo fucked me up something awful the past month. I don't even know why I bother," she explained.

Purdue was astonished at her resilience. By what he was told by her assistant she was in the final stages of Grade IV astrocytoma and that she could barely move or speak properly. Dismissing the information as exaggeration Purdue carried on the conversation as if he did not have any knowledge of her condition.

"I understand," he smiled. "You are a great deal more threatening than I imagined I would find you." Purdue glanced to the snobbish butler who stood in the door like a mannequin, holding a bottle of Dom Perignon.

"Ha!" she cried in amusement. "Healy is ex-SIS, I'll have you know, so he is not always such a gentle old pup…" she flung her head back to address the butler, "…hey, Healy?"

He merely nodded.

"Come, pour us some of that, will you?" she requested, while pulling a long slender cigarillo from her antique cigarette case. Purdue's eyes were glued to the artifact. It was sterling silver, hand crafted and definitely second hand. A symbol the shape of a backwards 'N' adorned the centre with a downward line vertically through it. While she placed it on the small lamp table he read the inscription beneath.

'Das Reich'

Lydia was skinnier than he recalled, which was to be expected of the illness, but the other properties of her behavior with remarkably peculiar. She spoke with precision in perfectly formed words, delivering cogent arguments with the butler. There was no sign, other than the visual, that she was even sick.

But how she appeared was quite another story. In typical fashion expected of the frail suffering cancer and its painful treatment, she wore a turban-like scarf around her balding head to cover the feathery remnants on her scalp. Her once ample lips were now deflated and contorted in wrinkles of agony she must have suffered thus far and her breasts had

27

disappeared almost completely. But those huge blue eyes under the dainty brow, falling slightly back into large eyelids were still unmistakable. Purdue remembered how deeply in love he was with her before she married Professor Graham Jenner in her late twenties and left him nursing several bottles of brandy and a broken heart.

"You fancy it, don't you?" she winked.

Embarrassed momentarily by her apparent reading of his mind, Purdue snapped out of his nostalgia, "I fancy what, dear Lydia?" His profuse blinking betrayed his discomfort at being discovered swooning over his old feelings for her. Lydia laughed heartily. With her aged, but still elegant finger she pointed to the silver cigarette holder. "You have a penchant for German war relics, do you not? I read about that somewhere. I think in a book or article by that sexy journalist, Sam Cleave."

'Sexy? Sam?' Purdue shouted in his mind. *'Hardly.'*

"Oh?" he replied. "He said that, did he?"

"Did you not read his book? I know it covered mostly his memoirs about exposing Whitsun's arms ring and the death of his fiancé and all that, but he mentioned that he was involved in the recovery of German World War II artifacts and religious relics with renowned explorer and inventor, David Purdue. Christ, Dave, the man is apparently one of your friends and you did not even bother to read his book?"

"I haven't had time," Purdue stuttered, aiming for the bottom of his glass. "Besides, I am not here to talk about Sam Cleave. I came to catch up with you, my dearest. Go on, tell me what you have been up to."

"Apart from hosting a war between God and a disease? Not much, really," she said serenely, blowing out a straight stream of smoke.

"Madam, with respect, you should not be smoking," Healy

reminded her, offering an ashtray for her to relinquish her cigarillo.

"With respect, Healy, fuck off," she chuckled crudely, almost malicious in her way. He looked briefly toward Purdue as if to ask for his help, and retired to the lobby to collect the dying bouquet for discarding. "Dave, take the cigarette case, darling. Soon I'll have no use for it anymore."

"So, you are quitting smoking," he smiled and took the item in his hand to run his fingers over the etching.

"No, I'm quitting living, you idiot," she bristled suddenly.

Purdue looked up at her in earnest and she quickly realized what she had done. Her tone had been utterly inappropriate, she knew. Contrite, she lowered her face, "I apologize. I really am sorry, Dave. It's just, so unfair what has happened to me. First I am left a widow and then this, you know. I am...oh Christ, I'm so sorry..."

"No need to excuse your words, Lydia," he said, almost placing his hand on her knee before remembering the sore skin she warned about. "It is natural to be angry."

"I am angry. I'm fucking furious, Purdue. And do you know why?" she said, abruptly lowering her voice.

"No?" he replied, truly intrigued. "Why?"

He knew Lydia Jenner all too well. She was always up to something, no matter what her situation. She was a hustler, a shaker, an inventor and genius who lived life only for one purpose – to seek. Incredulous to anything she could not substantiate with science, she always sought to discover the secrets of the universe or at least the possibilities of its arcane functions.

"Because I have stumbled upon something that works, my friend," she rasped in something between a whisper and a vulgar cackle. "Something that they theorize, all of them, while I actually attained the practical working of it! Sounds like witchcraft, doesn't it?" Her beauteous eyes addressed him with powerful terror, a sensation Purdue had only felt once before when he was in the presence of a Peruvian art dealer who was possessed by some sort of demon, some sort of psychological mishap that drove him mad.

"It does sound like witchcraft," he agreed inadvertently. "But do tell me more, dearest." Purdue did his best to hide his uncertainty by maintaining his flirtatious way she knew well from their days at Birmingham. It would keep her fooled long enough to share her madness with him, he reckoned.

She smiled satisfactorily and giggled. It was not a sweet sound at all, but rather a disturbing outlet of wisdom at a price, he thought. And it was. Lydia wanted something more than Purdue's company.

"Do you know where I got that cigarette case you like – you *covet* – so much?" she whispered with a malignant tone. "I got it from SS-Sturmbannführer Helmut Kämpfe himself, reportedly killed while in the custody of the French Resistance on 10 June 1944, or something. Stole Tesla's death ray notes from him, as well as this very cigarette case, right after I fucked his brains out."

For a moment she searched Purdue's face for a reaction, but his stunned expression at her confession was too much to bear, and Lydia burst out laughing like some uncouth whore. Purdue did not realize that her seemingly normal behavior was just the shaky shell to the severe damage inside her cranium, that she was in fact this far gone after all.

"You are kidding me!" he played along, clapping his palms together in faux-amusement. "How the hell did you achieve that?"

Lydia suddenly scowled, as if his believing her spoiled her fun. "Wait, you actually think I could do such a thing?" Her glass was shaking in her hand and Purdue took note of the clinking of cutlery in the dining room, wishing that Healy would just show up to distract her.

"Abso—…..absolutely. Of course I believe it. You, of all people, would be capable of designing something that could facilitate time-space manipulation," he explained, keeping up his charade under a ruse of nonchalance. "Besides, I would not put anything short of the Big Bang past you hand, dear Lydia."

She stared at him, her sunken cheeks drawing attention to the way in which she was grinding her teeth. A moment of uncomfortable silence passed before her frown vanished, but she was still not smiling. Instead she took on a more concerned persona.

"Dave, I need you to do something for me. I hate to admit this, but I did not invite you here to catch up on our lives before my body fails me for the last time," she said softly, cradling her tumbler and looking deep into the liquid. "I needed someone who was as bat shit crazy as I am..." she said, looking up at him, "...in the sense of scientific ruthlessness, of course. Someone like you would be insane enough to believe me, because you were always the one bloke who would never see obstacles, rather challenges; who would never tolerate perturbation of a theory or plan. Purdue, I need someone like you to finish my thesis and put it to practice as I could not."

Purdue was dumbfounded. She was actually serious about employing his loyalty to prove some ludicrous theory her illness allowed her to believe could be achieved in practice. His eyes blinked rapidly behind his small framed glasses and where his chin rested on his palm, his little finger probed his lips in thought.

"Please?" she whispered, marginally sane in her desperate beseeching. "Purdue, please. If it's the last thing you do for me."

Purdue had to concede that the small hint at what he thought she was onto enticed him no end, and knowing her boundless genius dampened only by her reputation as a dark horse in the academic community, the thought of what she had in mind was too good to rebuke.

"What do you need from me?" he asked seriously, his eyes narrow with warmth and amity. "Will it cost me my life this time?"

His jest fell lightly on her will. "If it did, Dave, your legacy would boast a feat no other man in history would ever have achieved." Her hoarse voice was filled with promise, gradually swallowing the madness inside it.

"Madam, do you wish to have a light meal with Mr. Purdue or shall we wait until formal dinner time?" Healy asked.

"Are you hungry, Purdue?" she asked abruptly. "It all depends on you. I don't get hungry anymore, it seems. Besides, I have to drink my food these days." Again came her wild cackling, harboring a furious admittance of defeat. "I'm like a fly, you see. I vomit. I consume liquid full of proteins and God knows what else they fill it with, only to grow uglier and deader by the day."

"Can't say that leaves me with much of an appetite, Lydia," Purdue cringed.

"Oh come on, Dave, don't be such a girl's blouse. Have some bloody food while you still can. Imagine I am eating with you. Healy is a hell of a cook," she insisted, swigging up the rest of her alcohol.

"Madam."

"Yes, Healy, my dear nurse maid. I know I am not allowed to drink. But if you don't tell, I won't...*kill you*!" she grinned, and flung the glass at her butler. It shattered against the wall just west of his cheek and he sank to his haunches to avoid the shrapnel of shards cleaving his face.

CHAPTER 5

*S*am unpacked his bag with savage indifference as the television behind him reported on the investigation lodged into the incident at CERN which derailed construction of the Alice detector. The latter was said to be part of the Large Hadron Collider, to record data from the mimicking of the Big Bang, taking pictures of the smashing of particles, so said the reporter. Yet, they still had no idea how the fire started and it still looked like an electrical short that could have been the cause.

Exhaustion was taking its toll on Sam, but he had to suck it up and pull himself together. To his annoyance as a free-lancer, the esteemed nitpicker Penny Richards went ahead and made an appointment with a CERN engineer, Albert Tägtgren, to be interviewed by Sam.

"I hope you don't mind," she told Sam. "I just thought you would get on faster if I located you the right people to speak to so that you won't waste your time trudging through the place looking for someone who could shed some light on the fire."

"That's fine, Penny, thank you. But how do you know

PRESTON WILLIAM CHILD

which people happen to know about the incident?" he asked her, aiming that cynical journalistic radar straight at her. But she was prepared for his astute nature.

"I don't reckon he would know who started the fire, Mr. Cleave, however as an engineer who specifically works on the Alice detector's structural resilience and construction, he would be best versed in what kind of structure the detector is build. Therefore, he might know better than anyone else where a fault could have arisen, had it not been arson," she rambled off, while Sam could not find one suspicious loophole in her explanation and ultimately had to respond with a simple, "Oh, alright then, Penny. I am heading out to CERN soon. I will Skype you this evening."

"Thank you so much, Sam," she replied cheerfully. "Have a lovely day."

He put the phone down. "Aye, I hope your day blossoms into a fervent frenzy of misery, you little gnat."

Sam had been imagining Penny as a gnat, specifically, since he made her acquaintance. Mentally he likened her to something seemingly insignificant and small that had an uncanny tendency to fly up one's air passages and wreak havoc. Not a deadly kind of havoc, just enough to spoil your day and make you extremely uncomfortable.

It was morning in Geneva. Breakfast was served and consumed without any enthusiasm from the Scottish journalist, and he shed all manner of cheer to prepare him for a boring day he just wanted to get behind him so that he could get Penny off his back and dive into the bottle of Scotch he had just purchased.

"Looking awfully downtrodden there, son," a familiar old voice came from behind Sam while he was having his last coffee after emptying most of his plate in the dining hall of his hotel. The distinct Dutch accent was unmistakable. Sam turned around.

34

"Professor Westdijk! What a pleasant surprise," he smiled for the first time that morning. The old man gestured for permission to join Sam at his table, his hands full of things – a mug of hot chocolate, a newspaper and a small plate with two slices of dry toast sliding about on the clean porcelain.

"I thought I would find you here, young Sam, but not this soon. I suppose you are here to probe that fire problem?" he asked as he drew his chair closer until his belly cushioned the table.

"Aye."

"I don't want to dissuade you, Sam, but I think you are fighting a losing battle. There are over two thousand scientists, engineers and electricians working on the construction of Alice, mostly British. There is not much chance you will get to speak to the right people before the trail goes cold," the old man remarked while he tried in vain to get the little rock hard block of butter onto his toast.

"It's funny you should mention that, Professor," Sam said, "…because I happen to have an appointment with someone I was pointed towards this very morning, for that very reason."

"Pointed? By whom, exactly?" Professor Westdijk asked, biting into the ridiculous morsel that clearly pained his gums.

Sam checked his notes, "Uh, one Albert Tägtgren?" Sam waited for the professor to light up and recognize the name, but he only nodded, chewing like a horse.

"And what does he do?" Professor Westdijk asked with his mouth full.

"I think he is a structural engineer involved in building Alice," Sam replied, still hoping there would be more detail behind the man he was to see.

"Nope, don't know him. It's a pity, because I know a lot of

people working on Alice," he told Sam, lifting his crooked finger to summon the waiter. "Earl Grey, please."

"What exactly do you do at CERN, if I may ask," Sam mumbled to avoid the waiter from hearing.

"I am just an advisor on the CMS…as soon as those inept assholes are done building the damn thing of course. There are about twenty five of us, physics experts in different practices, working on the detector. Most of them are from England and Germany. I am the only one from Holland," the professor explained. "But I hope you can figure out what happened to Alice. At least that would help the project along, otherwise everything will be put on hold to wait for the closing of the investigation before anything can continue. As you can imagine, with one giant circular tube in which the experiment is to be held, we need all components in running order before any of the other detectors can be activated."

"I understand," Sam said. In fact, he did not know exactly how the LHC was to operate, but the professor need not know that. "So everything is held up? I just hope I can get more detail on the electrical workings of the Alice detector, otherwise I will have no way of figuring this one out."

"Good luck," the old professor laughed, his cheeks dark pink and his goatee riddled with bread crumbs.

"You make it sound so much easier than my nightmares told me it would be," Sam smiled miserably, shaking his head.

"Agh, don't fret, Sam. In time this will also dissipate and what worries you today will be just a memory," the professor said, wiping his hands on his cardigan. Sam looked at his watch.

"Well, there are questions to be asked. I must dash, Professor. Thanks so much for the conversation. I don't feel so horribly out of place amongst the guests here now," he told the old scientist.

"I'll probably run into you there. Try not to get overwhelmed, alright? It's just a project. A multi-billion Euro project that will probably come to nothing but factions of physics professors at loggerheads about what they *actually* achieved by the experiment," the old man chuckled as Sam waved goodbye and left the hotel, ten minutes behind schedule.

SAM TOOK the time travelling to the CERN facility to enjoy the environment. From what he had learned in his research the construction companies had utilized the unearthed soil and gravel well, but employing the best functional landscaping to create a vast landscape of hillocks and small lakes to form a man-made park. It looked beautiful, with rolling mounds of green lawns and large bodies of water. The tall fence of the facility came into view along the road and Sam's stomach sank.

He hated to admit that he was not one for science or particle physics and he knew very little about mass construction and super machines. Now he would have to either maintain a ruse of knowledge or let everyone know that he, the great prize winning journalist, was now at the mercy of their tolerance in his ineptitude. Maybe he just felt that way because his life of late had been slightly off the norm. Of all the intense adventure he had survived, perhaps his life could only dip into boredom and lackluster, who knew.

"Credentials," the guard asked through the driver's window.

Sam showed the man his press pass and after a brief call to the office, the guard returned. "Section 8 only, Mr. Cleave. There is a restaurant in Section 8 for you to wait. Please do not venture off to any other part of the facility."

"Thank you," Sam replied.

As he expected, it was a maze of white coats and hard

hats that enveloped him as he searched for Section 8, where Albert Tägtgren would meet him.

"He is probably already waiting, pissed as hell," Sam muttered to himself as he searched the select few males seated alone in the huge spread of tables in the restaurant, which reminded him more of a mess hall one would find in Star Trek.

"Sam Cleave?" someone said.

"Aye," Sam almost shouted, elated that he did not have to go along asking every engineer-looking man his name. A very neat blond man appeared in front of him, extending a hand. He wore square glasses and his wedding band was the same color as his tie, Sam noted.

'Looks like a seventies serial killer to me,' Sam entertained himself in thought.

"Albert Tägtgren, at your service. Penny Richards told me you would be coming," he smiled cordially. Sam was relieved that the man with the Swedish accent was not pissed as hell after all.

"I'm sorry I am late, Mr. Tägtgren," Sam started.

"Please call me Al," the engineer told Sam. "Everyone calls me Al. It is less...Swedish?" He laughed and took Sam by the upper arm. "Coffee?"

"Oh, no thank you. I just had about a liter of caffeine at my hotel just to wake up. Long night of research," Sam explained, looking around at the chatting crowd of scientists and construction men.

"Research on CERN?" Al asked him.

"Afraid I still don't know everything I'm supposed to know," Sam admitted, choosing the honest, ill-informed path. But it was a good choice, because Albert Tägtgren was the kind of man who enjoyed enlightening laymen on his line of work. He spent the next two hours explaining structural engineering requirements and basically what the collider's experiments would entail. Sam's head spun with all the talk of the Higgs boson particle and the speeds at which the collider will propel particles to cause tiny crashes every few seconds, or so he understood the gibberish. Eventually Sam had to remind the over-zealous engineer what he really interviewed him about.

"So, after that bit of background," he said in his boyish teasing, "can you fill me in on the structural damage sustained during the recent fire?"

His host grew silent for a moment, not expecting that Sam had kept his focus through the entire lecture. Tägtgren cleared his throat and fumbled with his security card. First he surveyed the area as if he was about to share a secret... which he was.

"Mr. Cleave, I have a theory, but honestly I am too reluctant to voice it, especially to a journalist, you understand?" he said under his breath. Sam was very satisfied with the man's response.

"I understand completely. But if you want, we can keep this off the record," he assured Albert, switching off his recorder and putting it away. "I am far more interested for myself what the truth is, than to appease a bunch of business moguls looking to find a political scapegoat."

"Well, I am very happy to hear that, Mr. Cleave, but this is definitely not about politics or competition. In fact, it goes beyond the believable and dare I say, explainable," Albert whispered urgently.

CHAPTER 6

*P*urdue had his fill of the roast pork and asparagus, baby potatoes and creamed spinach Healy had prepared, but what he could not stomach was the erratic behavior of his hostess. By the evening he had begun to regret coming to see her, but something about her hints kept him at the gambling table. The wind howled outside the deathly quiet house. Morose and slightly unsettled, Purdue bided his time before thinking to excuse himself, but Lydia Jenner had way too much to get off her chest to just let her guest up and leave like that.

"Hurry up with that brandy, darling. I have to show you something," she told Purdue just as he set aside his dessert bowl and reached for the small glass Healy poured for him. He could not help but get a shiver from her words. It left him feeling oddly unsettled. Between Purdue and Healy many quick glances flashed when Lydia was not paying attention.

"As a point of interest," Purdue said, "why is there no music in this house? You used to love playing you vinyl's day in and day out."

"That is a lot of explaining that I cannot deliver until you

40

have seen what I wish to show you, old cock." She paused with an endearing smile, seeking the right words to start with. "You see, I cannot listen to music anymore. In fact, any sound louder than 40dB would be catastrophic," she explained casually.

Purdue had expected some long tirade, but this was the nature of Lydia Jenner. One could never predict her reaction to anything. The illness may have exacerbated her mood swings, but it certainly had not changed her personality. Healy did not say a word, but it was obvious that he knew many secrets about his employer.

"What I know about sound frequency is that this very conversation would already be around 60dB, Lydia. I think you have your numbers mixed up," he winked at her.

"No, I don't. Christ, how well do you know me, Dave? Would I make such a stupid claim if I was inaccurate about it?" she asked, raising her voice slightly. "Healy, I want Scotch."

Reluctantly the meticulous butler poured her a drink, his eyes dwelling to Purdue's, locking him in subliminal conversation.

"My apologies. I did not mean to make you out to be a fool, but really, nobody is perfect, dear Lydia. You could easily have misspoken, that's all," Purdue explained with his cheerful charisma perfectly in place to set her at ease.

"I have not...*miss...spoken*," she growled softly at him, and lifted the glass to her lips. When she swallowed, her eyes fixed on Purdue's like a predator to prey, Lydia put the glass down and slowly pulled aside the turban to reveal her ears. Flat steel discs were covering the shell of her ear, fixed to her head by what appeared to be a copper based strap that ran between the discs to secure it to her head, like headphones.

"Oh, my," Purdue replied in astonishment, or rather, fascination. He got up and stalked slowly toward Lydia, keeping his gaze firmly on the interesting device she wore. Lydia smiled, "Oh, darling, if you only know the rest."

"I would love to," he said softly. "What do these do?"

"They keep my skull from exploding every time someone speaks to me," she chuckled. "I designed them myself. Do you approve?"

"My goodness, this is a device to dampen the intensity of sound pressure without compromising the level, the volume. Am I correct?" he guessed, carefully reaching out to touch the contraption in sheer intrigue.

"That's right, Dave. Without it I would hear your voice like the clap of a shotgun with every word you utter," she revealed.

"But brain cancer does not do that, does it? I'm afraid I don't have much background in the illness itself," he admitted.

"No, it is not the cancer," she said. "It is part of why I asked you to come and see me, why I needed a madman with unsurpassed genius and boundless resources...you. Now, when you are quite done with that brandy..."

"I'm done," he interrupted her. His eyes glinted with exhilaration and even when he locked eyes with Healy, Purdue did not show any sign of relent. "Show me, Lydia. Show me everything you wish."

"Ohh," she giggled, "do you hear that, Healy? The man is almost horny for what I have. Only Purdue would have a boner for the science and not the scientist!" Again she unleashed the witchery in her laughter, but as before, the sound bounced back in dead air from the sheet lined walls. Purdue observed now that the entire manor was lined like the fence outside, hidden beneath paint and wallpaper.

With Healy pushing her wheelchair Lydia Jenner led Purdue into the innards of the mansion where it gradually became less of a home and more of a laboratory. Although it was not a proper place of experimentation, he noticed that she had converted spare rooms and hallways, showers and even broom cupboards into pallid and precise rectangular settings for the myriad of wiring, electronic devices, power boards and fat old computer monitors running in DOS. Apart from the meticulously arranged drawers and blinds over acoustic foam applied to every inch of the walls and ceiling, the place was a mess reminiscent of an electronic junk yard in the back of a radio store. As they advanced toward the last chamber, a walk in safe of sorts, Healy switched on the fluorescent lights that ran the length of the corridors and the circumference of the ceilings in every room. Some of the spare rooms had been altered, their west walls demolished to create one long room from the meeting of both spaces to accommodate machines Lydia had built.

Purdue was categorically ecstatic by the possibilities of what he perceived in Lydia's exquisite lunacy. His eyes combed the wiring, the technology and how it was arranged in relation to the strange sheeting.

"I know, it's a bit *steam punk*, is it not?" she smiled, watching his childlike fascination escalate. "I wanted to do it with the very caliber of materials it was theorized with."

"What?" he asked with his mouth agape at the sight of the retro experimentation space.

"I'm sorry, I don't understand," she frowned.

"Oh, I mean, what was theorized that you experimented with," he clarified.

"Well, there is not a name for it yet. I have not progressed much since…" she shot a glance up at Healy's wary eyes, "… the sickness happened."

"I see. And that is where you need me, I suppose?" Purdue asked eagerly. Lydia nodded, affirming his expectation. He looked at her rigid butler, but Healy deliberately kept his eyes and body language steady. It was the moment of truth.

His employer was about to reveal her plan to the man she told Healy was trustworthy, the billionaire who would apparently not steal her patents or take credit for her achievements.

Not for one moment did Healy neglect his task of paying attention to the stranger from Edinburgh. Lydia entrusted her butler with the unsavory task of snapping Purdue's neck if he even exhibited the need to steal her idea and make off with it. His meticulous nature was not exaggerated at all, in that he had already sent Purdue's driver home while he enjoyed the succulent roast. Dave Purdue did not know this, but he was to remain at Jenner Manor for a longer stay than he had anticipated.

"Now, tell me already," Purdue smiled, clasping his hands together as he always did when he was excited about an adventure.

"Come. See this chamber? It is called the *Voyager III,*" she smiled. She waited. Purdue waited for her to continue, but what she expected did not appear on his face. "Dave, do you know what the name denotes?"

Purdue looked at Lydia with a befuddled smirk of amazement. He knew what she was saying, but in his brilliant mind he could not calculate the possibility and plausibility rapidly enough to test her theory before agreeing with it. He stuttered, "It's a…time machine?"

Even as he uttered the words he felt a fool. What was he implying? Was he actually being gullible enough to believe that it had been accomplished? Then her words emerged in his recollection, the words she spoke when she smoked that first cigarillo.

'Do you know where I got that cigarette case you like – you covet – so much? I got it from SS-Sturmbannführer Helmut Kämpfe himself, after I fucked his brains out.'

Purdue knew as little about German history as the

average science geek, but one thing he knew for certain was that there was no way a forty seven year old woman could have encountered a Nazi officer in recent years, let alone rolled in the hay with him. It had to be true. And if any scientist could pull off such a stupendous feat it would be Lydia Jenner.

"I would not call it a time machine, per se," she smiled, admiring her work from the confinement of her wheelchair, "but you are on the right track. It employs Einstein's experimental unified field theory in part, adding in quantum gravity at a specific energy level."

"And it is able to bend spacetime?" Purdue gasped. "It can be done?"

She lolled her head to one side and shrugged, "With an extra punch of ..."

"You tease, Lydia!" Purdue cried impatiently.

"You might not believe this – a pinch of sound pulses, radio frequency at a specific amount of decibels. But that is still for me to know and you to feel awe for," she said quickly in a juvenile tone.

Purdue could not believe it. In his mind the numbers and formulas spun, diagrams formed and theories roiled, but he could not get it together. From what he knew, and it was much, Lydia's recipe could not possibly work. But that was something he elected to keep to himself until she could prove him wrong.

"So, what do you need from me?" he asked.

"I need you to accompany Healy to CERN. One of the CMS experiments will be conducted to detect miniature black holes," she explained.

"But I thought the particle accelerator would be utilized primarily for producing collisions by smashing together lead ions at tremendous energy levels," Purdue argued. "They intend to create a model where those collisions generate unprecedented temperatures, a thousand fold the heat of the centre of the Sun. Unless Alice or Atlas or one of the other detectors were saddled with black holes and dark matter and such."

Lydia's face contorted in a malicious intolerance, but she tried her best not to lose her temper with Purdue's argument. She needed him to complete her experiments.

"That is of no consequence to me, Dave. Please!" she shouted, but recovered her composure. "Forget about what the media knows about CERN's intentions with the LHC machines, okay? Jesus, my time is running out! I am in no shape – or mood - to engage in petty lectures."

Her voice was less aggressive, although it maintained its intensity. What Purdue heard was desperation, the desperation of a dying woman.

"I'm sorry, Lydia. You must understand that this is a lot in a short time to bombard me with. Please, carry on," he said, enfolding her shaking hands in his.

"My machine, the Voyager III, this one, needs a secondary capacitor that you will be able to find at the Alice. The one I used fried when I..." she hesitated, finding strength in Healy's static serenity, "...when I last tested it."

"You actually went back in time?" Purdue asked without expecting a reply. His smile was evident of his admiration and he kissed Lydia's gossamer skin on the back of her bony hand.

"I'll share a secret. Nikola Tesla, as you may know, was a Nazi sympathiser. But what always eluded Himmler was Tesla's design and notes on the theories of the *death ray*. I stole it from Himmler and his dogs by engaging Helmut but when I had to get back to 2013 I had no time to collect the notes from where I stashed them before my time window closed at the time, you see?"

"My God, Lydia."

Dave, do this for me and I will give you a 20% allotment, a share in credit and profit from any successful patent. Besides, once I am dead, my executors would still make sure you get yours. I'm good for it," she promised.

Dave Purdue had every reason to breach the law and rules for her. Financial gain was the least of his cares, but if he was part of the most monumental discovery in history, his name would be up there with the masters – Einstein, Planck, Galileo, Freddy Mercury, Archimedes, Elvis....

His addition of the musicians was just his whimsical whimsy, for fun.

"Purdue!"

He snapped out of it, "I'm in."

CHAPTER 7

No more than twenty minutes after Sam put away his recorder, he found himself inside the compound where the detectors were being assembled. It was break time for most of the engineers, so they did not pay much attention to the unfamiliar face that walked with Albert Tägtgren.

"Don't look so worried, Sam. There are so many multinationals working on this experiment that new faces are common around here every now and then," the engineer smiled. He had Sam decked out in a coat and hard hat, complete with a clipboard and pencil, the reason for which escaped Sam completely, but he was not about to complain being smuggled into a section that was not marked with an '8'.

"If I get discovered…" Sam whispered.

"You won't, unless you act like a journalist or something. Right?" Al reminded him. "Now follow me as if you have been here before. Mind the third step. We all here know the third step is narrower than the others, and now you do too."

"Right-o," Sam replied, and loosened up a bit.

They headed toward the Alice detector, said a few hellos to the rival teams of scientists, with Al stopping occasionally, pretending to discuss circuits or concrete density with Sam. Along the main lines they moved until they entered a small space between the wall and the power boards. Sam could still smell it. The nauseating stench of the electrical fire permeated around them, that awful rubbery residue that settled in one's throat.

"This is where it happened?" he asked Al.

The engineer nodded seriously, checking that they did not draw unnecessary attention.

"This is where the fire stopped. It started somewhere inside the tube. What is baffling is that the actual experiment is only due to start later this year, but what we saw was," he swallowed hard and frowned, "not normal. I don't want to sound like one of those people on UFO documentaries, Mr. Cleave, but I saw a man catch fire and then he was gone."

"Wait, wait, wait," Sam exclaimed, feeling distinctly spooked by the imagery Albert conveyed to him. He placed his hand flat on the engineer's chest and shook his head profusely. "Just...run that by me again. Slowly."

"Off the record."

"Aye, off the record, but don't leave out anything," Sam urged.

"I was one of seven engineers and electricians who came to inspect the two new installations we did that day. You see, we must make sure the wiring that the electricians lay are properly secured in the casings and supported according to the weight and dimension requirements," Albert started in his hindering English. Sam was dying to move him along, but he did ask for detail, after all. In his pocket, his finger had pressed down the *record* button on his audio recorder, but his expression remained unchanged.

"And then?" Sam pressed.

"We heard a loud clap and then the sound of currents, electrical currents, a few meters down the tube. There was a separate slice lying on its side. I'll show you now. Come, let's go," he told Sam, pulling him by his sleeve deeper into the damaged tube to where the blackened steel remains of a pod-like structure lay sprawled like a giant dead spider.

"See? There. That was a container that carried and stored a lot of generators and conductors, copper wiring and capacitors. But when we saw lighting currents come from it we raced to see what was happening. Arcs of blue lightning shot from it and when we came here, see…?" he pointed to the open side of the semi-circular container, "…we saw a human figure that was, what's the word? Alight? Alluminated?"

"Illuminated," Sam corrected him.

"That's right. It was so quick, but we all saw it. When the capacitors ran out of energy the arc stopped and the figure caught fire. But Sam, it was a fire like we have never seen! It looked like a space shuttle's reentry into the atmosphere, a sort of burn through. The next thing we knew the body had vanished into the fire, like he stepped into thin air!" Albert exclaimed, hardly realizing that his relation was growing louder. Sam hushed him.

"And then the place caught fire too?" he asked Al.

"Yes. That fire around his body vanished with him into thin air, just like that," Al said, motioning with his hand in front of his mouth and blowing it away. "But them the fire came back, I swear to God! It just came right back out of the nothingness and spread like an explosion. All we could do was run for our lives! By the time we reached the other side of Alice, the whole section was burning like a wildfire."

"Jesus. Did anyone get hurt? The media reported that this happened during a late shift, fewer people…" Sam asked.

"Yes, it was late. But our superiors did not want the true nature of the blaze to come out in the media. You know, we have enough crap with the protestors and local opposition groups about what we are trying to accomplish here, you see?" Al rambled as the pungent smell got the better of Sam.

"Can we get out of here? I'm getting sick from this smell," he asked the engineer.

"Sure. Sure," Al replied, leading Sam back out from the hideous black scene, "but you won't leak this, right? Remember, if it comes out I'll know who leaked it."

"Really?" Sam marveled as he used his coat to cover his nose and mouth. "Really? You still have time to deal me a threat?"

Albert shrugged, "It's a very serious issue. I just had to tell someone. I don't know why I trust you. I know I shouldn't."

"No, you shouldn't. But I'm not a complete bastard. If this comes out...IF...no-one will ever know where it came from. There were seven of you. It could be any of you, right?" Sam reminded him.

"You are going to tell this?" Al shouted, exasperated at the journalist's betrayal.

"Relax! No, I'm going to use your information to figure out what really happened," Sam reassured him.

"I just told you what really happened!" Al persisted.

Sam calmed him down and pulled him aside. In a hushed tone he told Al what he meant. "Look, I know what you saw, but I need to know why this happened and who the man was that caught fire. Where he is now and who he worked for, what he did to make this happen – all that. That is what I am here to address. So stop fretting. Your identity is safe."

Sam's explanation seemed to calm the nervous engineer.

"Nothing strange has happened since, right?" Sam asked.

"No," Al replied, at once seeming dead tired and worried. "Nobody has come near that mess since they extinguished it. They are waiting for the marshals to submit a report to see if it was arson or an electrical fault before our people are allowed to clean up and write up the cost of the damaged." He looked to the ground and shook his head. "Fucking millions lost," he sighed.

"I don't suppose you will let me take pictures of the container," Sam appealed to Albert's favor.

"No," the engineer summarily dismissed the request out of hand. "There is no way. Telling you the story is one thing, but pictures would be actual proof, actual evidence. I'll get fired."

"Alright, alight," Sam yielded. "Well, thank you so much for the information, Al. It was good of you to trust me with your story, but as I said, please don't worry about me leaking this, alright?"

"Okay," Al replied, looking a bit more relieved.

"Um, I know my way out, but I just have to pee. Can you direct me to the nearest men's room?" Sam asked.

"Of course. Sure," Al said and took Sam to the Section 4 area rest rooms before he said goodbye.

Sam rushed into a cubicle in the empty rest room. Inside he quickly drew the recorder from his pocket and slid it into the back pocket of his jeans. From his satchel he took his GoPro, fully charged the night before.

"Who said size matters?" Sam jested as he wrapped the tiny video camera in his palm. "Can't believe he actually thought I would leave before getting footage. Super intelligence does not make you smart, does it, old Al?" Sam smiled as he reinvented his scientist look, complete with his fake spectacles. The hard hat he would have to steal from one of the stations, but with night drawing near it would hopefully be easier.

Finally he was satisfied that he looked the part for blending in and slipped out towards the restricted section they had come from.

'Thank God I have a keen sense of direction. This fucking maze

would confuse anyone who doesn't work here every day,' he thought as he navigated his way. He checked his watch. It was late already and although they worked around the clock, the people who had seen his face already were all about to knock off from their shifts. He was pressed for time nonetheless. Soon the security guards would be alerted that the visitor was still in the facility and over his time limit. Not to mention that he was about two kilometers away from the only section he was allowed in.

Sam moved with groups of people, staying just far enough behind them to look like he was part of the section, but not too close. He did not want them to discover him before he could at least get some sort of evidence to feed Penny Richards and her foundation. Besides that, he was intrigued about Albert's story, but whether he was completely convinced of the authenticity of the story was still a matter for consideration.

After a nerve wrecking trek through strangers who knew one another in corridors that all looked the same Sam finally recognized the place where he and Al greeted the scientists and engineers. They were scattered now, dealing with their respective problems in the construction and assembly of the giant machines. Sam pretended to check some circuits while glancing towards the Alice detector's damaged section, planning his next move to advance. Some of the plumbers and maintenance personnel gave him suspicious looks, but they were uncertain of their judgment. Maybe he was just a new scientist from one of the more obscure countries involved in the project. They did not have the time to make it their business anyway.

When Sam checked the charred section behind the tape barriers again he saw something move right there in the vicinity of the container. His heart jumped. With all this talk of men disappearing into thin air he was caught between fascination and skepticism, yet there was an inkling of possibility to it that kept Sam interested – and foolishly brave. If caught he could face serious charges, including espionage or sabotage and that would certainly have costly consequences for him.

Again there was some movement behind the circuit boards just short of the one opening on the container. Sam darted quietly towards it, his camera activated to capture whatever was there. As he crossed the tape barrier he knew he was onto something. There was a shape moving in the blackness. Sam snuck around the side of the pod to see when a mighty blow to the head struck him down, sending his camera sliding across the concrete.

His eyes burned and his skull felt as if it was mounted on roll bolts, stinging into his neck from the harsh impact, but he was conscious. Two figures stood over him, blurred and mumbling. When his vision improved through his fake glasses he caught his breath.

"Purdue?"

CHAPTER 8

*L*ydia drew in the marijuana vapor, filling her lungs leisurely.

"Hmm, home grown is best," she groaned in her hoarse tone, smiling to herself.

Her eyes rolled back in their sockets as she did, and the silence of the house loomed over her like a fast approaching stalker with no good intentions. Her mind raced with ideas, consequential concern, old memories, regrets and somewhere among the rush of her mind, the date of her death. It was an enigma, yes, but she knew it would be soon.

In the privacy of her own bedroom she waited for the men to return with that one elusive component she needed. She would have sent Healy, but the man was a soldier, a mercenary, not a scientist. Purdue, on the other hand, not only possessed the necessary aptitude for what she needed, but he had a passion similar to hers. Truth was that Lydia saw Purdue as her stuntman, her stand-in now that she could not even take a piss by herself without great pain and discomfort.

Healy was her only employee, save for the maids that

came in twice a week. To them she was just another well paying client. They pitied the temperamental lady for her terminal condition and that was just the way Lydia wanted it. Only her butler knew what was really going on and he was the only person in Lyon she trusted. Now he was one of only two people she entrusted with her secrets, the other being old friend Dave Purdue.

Her room was quite different from the rest of the house, although it still featured the sheeting. Without these special walls she would perish from even the slightest fluctuation in sound, yet this was not something she could tell Purdue yet. It could spook him into abandoning his loyalty for fear of what could happen - the same thing that happened to her before. Facing her hideous reflection in her dressing table mirror, she slowly removed her head scarf and surveyed the surface of her scalp. Her hands lightly probed at the cotton wool patches of what was left of her hair, drawing a flood of silent tears from Lydia.

Sobbing softly in the deathly silence she reminisced about her fleeting time and her lost beauty.

"Was it all worth it?" she asked her reflection. "Well, was it?"

Lips moved under the tears of her image, but it lent her no answer. Her eyes fell to the pointless hair brush on her dresser and her heart grew taut with rage. Picking it up, Lydia played with the soft brush between her long lean fingers, nails painted to maintain some sort of vanity where the brittle condition had to be hidden. Even if she knew it was there, she need not see it.

"You'll see, Lydia. You'll see that it was worth it!" she shouted in her wicked rasp of defeat. "You will die, yes, but you will die having fucked the science world that rejected your genius!" Her watery, pink eyes grew wide and furious as she raised the brush at the impotent image of her crumbling face, "But are you willing to kill your friends for the glory? What if Purdue does not survive it? What if..." she seethed in her indecision, painfully plucking tufts of useless hair from her scalp.

This was Healy never left her alone. He knew of her emotional turmoil, a natural, but dangerous quality of her illness. "Look at you! You stupid glory whore! Are you happy now? Is this what you wanted? You are a dying piece of flesh with a voice, while your brilliant brain is shriveling up like a raisin!" she shrieked so loud that her skull shuddered and ached under the dangerous sound level of her cries.

Lydia caught her breath and held it.

Staring at herself in the mirror, shivering in a vicious rout, brush aloft in an unstable hand. The fading beauty contemplated her next action.

"Will it kill me? Shall we see? It is not like anyone would notice that a has-been bitch is gone. They'll find the poor little cancer victim on the floor, dead, where she belongs. Pity, pity, pity," she giggled in a girly voice, a true exhibition of what she had to contain and control in company – the fact that she was already insane.

Without another thought she hurled the hair brush into the large old mirror. It shattered the center of the looking glass, right where her face was. But that was by no means the worst. The crashing sound was too much for the plating on the walls to absorb, and the discs on her ears could only dampen some of the intensity.

Lydia screamed in pain as the sound screeched through her delicate brain matter. Her fragile body fell limply to the side from the numbing agony as she held her ears. But even that hurt.

"Oh Jesus! Jeeezussss!" she squealed, partly disappointed that the sound did not kill her instantly. The contact of her hands on the deteriorating skin of her ears and scalp was excruciating beyond her expectations. Her cellular degeneration had a severe effect on her nerve endings, more than she knew.

"It would be better not to fall out of your wheelchair now! No time to be melodramatic, you stupid, stupid bitch!" she growled inside the little space between her face and her knees, where she had buried her face as she writhed. The decibels still echoed in her ears, the pretty and brutal clinks of the mirror slivers falling one by one to the dresser.

When it all passed and Lydia's environment was quiet once more, she took a deep breath and sat up. Her image was wonderfully distorted in front of her. Lydia smiled.

"Finally your image becomes your fate," she smiled. Tears dried just short of her jaw line, but her eyes drowned.

CHAPTER 9

*J*n proper fashion to compliment the gaining madness in Lydia's mind, aided by the strange empty mausoleum she took residence in, the heavens dressed in grey. Occasionally the flashes of the electrical charges therein lit up Lyon's buildings and illuminated the beautiful winding Rhône that ran through the old buildings of the French city. She had recovered from her destructive act, but she was out of a personal mirror and had to explain the unholy mess in her room to Healy when he returned.

Lydia oddly felt obliged toward her butler. Yes, she acted as though he was her lackey, her servant and babysitter, but in all honesty she respected him a great deal. It was not that she was afraid of what he could do at all, but his silent and continuous loyalty was something she valued immensely. Often Lydia wondered what kind of lover he was, but she would never tarnish their perfect mutual devotion to find out. Besides, she was not half the alluring stunner she used to be and she would never expect a man like him to ever find someone like her desirable. Sometimes, when she watched him create order in the house from the hidden shadows

Lydia wondered if he remembered how beautiful she was before…before the illness came.

The door clicked loudly, but there was no echo. A blunt sound died less than three centimeters away from the lock, yet Lydia could hear it with the aid of her ear pieces. Her heart jumped from excitement. She wondered if they procured the capacitor without incident from the CERN laboratory and made work of wheeling herself arduously toward the lobby.

Lydia stopped in her path when the door opened.

There was Purdue and Healy, but they were accompanied by a very attractive man about he own age, nursing a bruise on his cheek.

"And? Did you get it?"

"Yes, madam," Healy replied, looking rather laid back as opposed to his usual stiffness. "This is Sam Cleave, by the way. He is a friend."

"Says who?" she scowled. "I don't know him!"

"He is a close friend and partner in crime, Lydia, of mine," Purdue explained.

The dark eyed man with the wild black hair nodded courteously. "Pleasure to make your acquaintance, Professor Jenner."

Lydia decided to like him.

"Sam, is it?" she asked.

"Aye."

"Scottish?" she asked again.

"Aye," he smiled. Lydia really liked him now.

"My husband was Scottish," she winked.

"I'm Scottish too!" Purdue reasoned amusedly.

"Yes, yes. But he is…new," she grinned.

Sam smiled and nudged Purdue mockingly. Lydia laughed, "Come on, Sam. We have a proper sick bay here in the manor. Let Healy treat that bruise for you."

"Madam," Healy began his protest, but to no avail.

"Healy. Take Sam to the infirmary and put something on that bruise that you no doubt caused!" she ordered. She knew her butler far too well. He obliged.

"Come with me, Sam," he told the journalist, leaving Lydia with Purdue.

"How are you feeling, beautiful?" he smiled.

Lydia wanted to be cynical about it, but she had had enough of her own antagonism for the evening.

"I'm doing well, thanks Dave," she winked amicably. "How did it go?"

"Easier than I thought. I retrieved a proper plate for you. Not the one you wanted…"

"Dave, I needed that specific storage plate!" she panicked.

"Hey, no worries, my dear Lydia. What I am trying to tell you is that I stole a higher aptitude device than the meager one you thought you needed!" Purdue explained boastfully. "Look."

He showed her the capacitor he had obtained from the Alice detector when nobody was watching him raid their storage units. "See? High intensity, extra storage of higher energy than the one you directed us to at Alice. The good thing is, when we ransacked the Alice reserves we found Sam. And all that without Healy having to distract the gentlemen and ladies of the workforce based adjacent to us."

Lydia felt better. Suddenly she felt as if she was surrounded by a whole army of allies. The men involved were all caring, intelligent and willing to help her. The only thing she lamented was the possibility of sacrificing them in the name of science. Not one, but all.

The latter would only be thwarted should she elect to end her own life instead, but Lydia was still reluctant to abandon her mortal vessel before she knew if the price was worthy of the reward. In her anticipation she could not imagine having to wait until morning, but she had to surrender to propriety and let the men settle in, get some rest and prepare for the tests of the new day to follow.

It pained her that she could not order them to march on down to the Voyager III at that very moment and prove to her, once and for all, that her capitulation to a greater force was not in vain after all. But as a good hostess she joined them in light banter in the drawing room after Sam's cheek was given some ointment and Purdue's curiosity was reined in in lieu of social interaction. He had to yield to the night and its relaxing activities and it was easier once he had made peace with the fact that he would have the run of the chamber and its curious components when he rose from bed the next morning.

Sam was just grateful that for once he was in a place of lodging with at least one familiar face and voice to put him at ease. Still he knew he had a good, diluted report to concoct to appease Richards and her foundation in the morning, but there were a dozen hours and an equal amount of whiskey glasses between now and then.

CHAPTER 10

*I*n the morning after breakfast Sam spent about an hour to prepare a proper report for the Cornwall Institute, although he made a solid effort to stretch the truth and embellish the unassuming into something ordinary and accidental. He told Richards and her people that the fire was caused by electrical short and that there was no reason to assume that any deliberate act or sabotage was involved.

"Are you ready, Sam?" he heard Purdue sing from the other side of the guest room's door.

"Shortly. I just need to send through this e-mail to get the Cornwall Institute off my back. I'll meet you down in the lab in a few minutes," he called back.

"Alright. Make it quick. You would not want to miss this, mate!" Purdue shouted as his footsteps hastened away from the door.

Sam uploaded the video footage from his encounter with the Alice engineer and the bit of video he obtained of the burnt metal before Healy's fist found him.

"Thank God he didn't break my camera," he sighed under his breath as he save the last clip to the laptop. He got up and rummaged through his messy bag of clothes. "Jesus, I need a laundry service," he mentioned quietly as he tried to find a shirt that was not hideously crumbled and creased.

A knock at the door solved his problem. Shirtless, wearing last night's less than clean jeans, he perked up.

"Mr. Cleave, it's Healy. Are you alright?" the butler asked.

"Aye! I'm fine, Healy," Sam replied, hatching a plan to sort out his wardrobe glitch. Gathering his only three shirts he went to answer the door. When he opened the door Sam was instantly humbled by the strict man's impeccable dress sense. Sam cleared his throat, "Excuse me for being forward, Healy, but can you get this ironed for me? I have nothing else with me and this looks awfully untidy."

Healy looked down at the shirts. "Very well, sir." He took the shirts from Sam and started down the corridor, but he suddenly stopped and turned. "Um, Mr. Cleave."

"Aye."

"Not to be brash, but those pants you are wearing should really join this bundle, don't you think?" Healy said plainly, pointing at Sam's jeans.

Slightly embarrassed, Sam leaned in to the butler and said softly, "I'm terribly ashamed to admit this, Healy. But I did not know that I would be away from home this long…or that I would end up on the ground at some point…"

Healy looked contrite for decking Sam to the floor at CERN.

"…so I have to admit that these are the only pants I have here."

DOWNSTAIRS PURDUE and Lydia were exchanging ideas on how the Voyager III should be set up for optimal performance.

"For the most efficient energy propulsion, I would replace the RI derivative completely, cut it out," he suggested.

"But then we have one less component to generate the necessary temperatures. We'll never be able to accelerate enough in the given time, Dave. We need all the energy sources we can use," she argued.

Looking at the schematic, they were lurching over the desk on the other side of the Voyager III. Only a double assembly stainless steel sound barrier wall with a small bullet proof triple plated observation window separated them from the subject inside the chamber – which Purdue had agreed to be for experimentation purposes.

From deep in the corridor they heard Sam and Healy approach.

"It's about time!" Lydia cried without looking up. "We are running out of time. There is a powerful storm coming and I don't want to run the risk of a lightning strike to fry the circuits. I am not trying to bring a stitched up dead monster come to life. I just want to test a theory."

Purdue chuckled, "You are far more alluring than Dr. Frankenstein, my dearest!"

Lydia smiled and winked at him. Purdue had always been a flamboyant flirt and she loved it. Doubt filled her about sending him into the chamber, but he was the perfect subject. With his knowledge of this field of study he was the best scientist to send in. After all, with his own theses on Einstein's arguments to relativity theory and the further perpetuation of quantum gravity this experiment would profit his own studies greatly. Who better than someone like Purdue to observe first-hand the workings of scientific prin-cipals he had only found tangible on paper. The paradox had to be shattered.

"Oh my God, Sam," she head Purdue exclaim. Lydia was curious as to his uttering and peeked around the tall, lean inventor to see Sam wearing Healy's chino's and polished shoes. The shirt he wore was extremely unlike what she guessed was normally Sam's style, but it worked with the ensemble. A tight fitting black t-shirt, slimming style in acrylic and nylon, strained across the journalist's chiseled chest and gave the impression that his biceps were twice the size they really were.

Lydia gave him a wolf whistle while Purdue applauded.

"Thank you, Healy," Sam called out as he forced a modeling gait. Healy could not help but sport a proud little smirk at his achievement of bailing out Lydia's guest with some of his own garb. Once they have settled down and Purdue had switched on the machine to power up over the next twenty minutes, Lydia pointed out the details to them.

"Sam, are you getting this?" Purdue asked, and Sam nodded, pointing his camera to the inventor and his lady friend.

"Please do not film the schematic, Sam," Lydia implored. "Only the effect of the experiment, yes?"

"Don't worry, Professor. I am not filming any intellectual property," he reassured her.

"Good. Now, Dave, these are the theoretical co-ordinates of what the machine is going to concentrate the power beam on. When we add the last component you will hear a loud crack, like a gunshot. That is when you should start paying attention," she instructed. Her excitement was obscured by her urge to get everything just right.

Lydia's voice was shivering slightly, exhibiting her appre-hension. Her time was running out and there were only so many chances at getting all the right ingredients in the quan-tities for her recipe. Her oven could only rise to the occasion with the most rigorous scientific power sources or else this cake would be a flop.

To the left of the schematic there was a dental cast freshly made, but Sam chose not to ask. He kept his movement undetected as much as he could as not to interfere or distract as he filmed the entire preparation process. Purdue did not seem at all nervous through Sam's view finder.

'You daft son of a bitch,' Sam thought. *'Anything for a thrill. Anything to be the first and the best, hey?'*

Purdue's awkward posture gave him a more twisted appearance over the fragile frame of the small woman next to him. They looked like two characters from an old black and white film about ghouls, Sam thought. And to make it more authentic through his eyes they were in actual fact discussing the impossible in a science lab. How apt it was!

"Right!" Lydia said finally, shifting the large worn paper aside. "That is all you have to know before you go in. Healy! One last drink before we embark on the most brilliant…"

"Dangerous," Sam muttered in between.

"…experiment ever attempted. The new and improved formula!"

"Hear, hear!" Purdue grinned. Lydia wheeled her chair to the sound proof cover on the other side of the altered spare room. Sam halted his recording and nudged Purdue, "Are you sure you want to do this?"

"Why, naturally, Sam," Purdue answered. "This is unprecedented!"

"That is precisely what is worrying me," Sam whispered with intense urgency. "If this goes wrong, if anything is one iota too little or too much, you will be electrocuted, Purdue! Dead fucking meat! Is that getting into your thick skull at all?"

"Yes, it is," Purdue said. The tranquil nature of his response disturbed Sam even more. He sounded almost indifferent.

"This is an uncontrolled experiment in someone's basement! The chance of success is meager and more than that, it is suicide," Sam pressed.

"Sam, this basement was constructed by one of the most exceptional minds in modern times. Besides, all virgin experiments are somewhat uncontrolled, aren't they? Nobody knew what fire could be used for at first," he whispered to Sam as he watched Lydia adjust the plating. "The Wright Brothers did not know if their craft was actually going to fly...until they risked it. Nothing would ever be discovered if people were too wary of the risk factor, Sam. Nothing."

"God forbid anything goes awry, what do I tell people?" Sam persisted, appealing to Purdue's personal issues in desperation. "What do I tell Nina?"

Purdue's light blue eyes stared at Sam from behind the enforced glass of his spectacles. He was quiet, in contemplation of Sam's words.

"That is a low blow, old boy," he replied at last. "Don't use Nina as some bargaining chip between my quest for discovery and my quest for love."

"Come, boys! It's time!" the raspy order came from Lydia. Between the two men the momentary stand-off spell snapped like a rubber band and they both returned to the task at hand. Sam had his camera rolling again and Purdue went into the changing booth to dress himself for the occasion. He removed his shoes and shirt. In his socks and vest he stood for a minute, listening to the humming current that flowed though the copper veins of the machine. Sam's warning suddenly became very real, uncomfortably sensible.

But if he backed out now and Lydia nailed the experiment with someone else he would regret it forever. He slipped on the brown overalls and stepped into the combat boots that were reinforced with rubber and asbestos. Over his white hair he slipped the tan leather aviator cap, feeling like an idiot as he fastened the straps with plastic press studs under his chin.

"Oh, don't forget to remove your glasses, Purdue. I have some tinted goggles here for your eyes to protect them against the light flashes of the surges," Lydia called out to him.

"Alright," Purdue replied.

'As if I did not look stupid enough already,' he thought, shoving his business writing pad into his boxers. On it he had noted the important information such as names and dates he was to keep track of to find what Lydia sent him for – hypothetically.

"You have to hurry," she pushed, beginning to sound rather whiny. "There is a storm due later this afternoon and I want this machine switched off by then. Let's do this already!"

Sam did not like the sound of the machine that was already removed from his favor by its makeshift construction, especially in consideration of the feat expected of it. To him the Voyager III was like a rusted old Volkswagen employed to race in Monaco's Grand Prix. He hatched an idea.

"Lydia, tell us laymen, where would the tentative co-ordinates send someone, should the Voyager III be capable of time travel?" he asked.

He feigned interest in her theory, but Lydia did not notice. An interview from a renowned journalist such as Sam Cleave was an ego booster, blinding her with vanity so that she did not realize that he was simply trying to probe at the depth of her delusion.

"In theory," she attempted to sound modest, just in case the model folded, "Purdue would have ended up where I last..." she suddenly stopped and deliberately coughed profusely so that she could formulate an answer that would not betray her secret before continuing.

"Do you need some water?" Sam asked. Lydia nodded. He put the camera down and ran to the bathroom next to the chamber room. By the time he returned she had sorted out her words. Drinking the entire contents of the glass, she inhaled deeply.

"Thank you, Sam."

He picked up the camera again and she explained, "As I was saying, he would probably arrive in 1944 here in France. I picked the date and location from an old document I once read that intrigued me about…"she seemed indifferent to the details, "…about, uh, I think Nikola Tesla's involvement in Nazi propaganda or something. Anyway, I used those settings, but as you realize it is only a point of reference."

"Of course. Of course that makes sense," Sam agreed. But his interview was cut short by Purdue's appearance, spoiling Sam's idea to stall long enough for the predicted storm to come before they could have the chance to do the experiment. But it looked like his well intended procrastination was run down by Purdue's zeal to make history.

CHAPTER 11

*A*t CERN the day was drawing into an atmosphere as volatile as the weather.

Albert Tägtgren rushed through the large crowd of white coats and hard hats to get to the main office to take a call. He had just arrived for his shift, but his superior told him that there was an urgent message for him to call the Cornwall Institute in connection with a bursary for his son.

"Go on, Al. Just make sure you get back here before Greenley knocks off. I need at least one structural engineer at Alice at all times," his superior told him before he headed for the office. He could not use his cell phone, for security reasons.

Fortunately the staff and workers at the laboratory were of such a vast number that nobody really kept up with anyone else unless they were close friends. Albert's colleagues did not know that he had no son and that the Cornwall Institute did not give bursaries. In fact, they did not know what the Cornwall Institute was. But Albert did. He also knew that the message was code for an urgent request to fix a problem.

"Miss Richards, it is Albert Tägtgren."

"Albert, did you speak to Sam Cleave yesterday?" she asked.

"Yes, ma'am. I told him what I knew and then he left," Albert said.

"Good. We do have one problem, though. We have reason to believe that there are more than a few moles in your section, so we would like you to listen and observe, see if anyone is acting strangely. We have a lot of money invested in this mission, so we cannot afford to have more hold ups by our opposition, understand?" she told the engineer.

"I will. So far I have not detected any odd doings," he reported.

"Just stay on your toes. Time is running out on all levels, so you know that soon something, somewhere, will transpire. The closer we get to the activation of the Super Collider the more trouble we can expect to surface," Penny reminded him with a tone of warning, fraught with worry. "And please don't let anyone guess at your true reasons for being there, Al. You would be in deep trouble if they knew that you were involved in the Tesla Experiment."

"Yes, Miss Richards. Don't worry. Nobody has any idea what I am doing here," he comforted her concerns. He ended the call with a renewed worry about the facts he gave that Scottish journalist the day before. Albert could kick himself for his cavalier disclosure of such a sensitive matter, but he could not help himself. Never before had he been in such an important position or known such weighty things and it felt good to be able to tell the secret. To share such an awe inspiring fact such as witnessing someone employ quantum mechanics in front of his eyes was just too much of a temptation. Besides, the journalist did not take pictures or film him, so there was always the comfort that he could deny anything Cleave placed on him, although Penny Richards would get word of it without a doubt, and he would be fired by the Institute.

"Tägtgren!" the Alice head engineer shouted. For a brisk moment Albert's guilt ridden heart stopped in fear of having been discovered. "Quick, come with me!"

"What is the matter, sir?" the covert engineer asked.

He walked with the head of the section's staff as the man went on about bad security and how his hide was up for tanning now. "I'm going to be in some deep shit, my friend. I hope you know what happened here of we are going to have a bloody media mess on our hands!"

"What happened?" he asked again as they approached the remnants of the burnt mess behind the security barriers where Tägtgren remembered showing the secret evidence to the journalist.

His heart pounded. The fact that he did not know what was amiss was almost worse than knowing how guilty he was of abetting the trespassing journalist. He lamented Penny Richards sending the man in the first place he would not have had to suffer this sheer stress. Why did she have to send Sam Cleave to probe the secret just so that she could find out how probable discovery of the true story would be by the media? Richards reckoned that, if a potent investigative journalist like Cleave could not figure out what really caused the fire, then the Institute's secret was safe against the lesser media vultures.

Now *he*, Albert Tägtgren was in hot water from all sides, because what Penny Richards did not know was that he was a double agent. The opposition of the Cornwall Institute paid better and they were aware that he worked for Penny, so he had no fear of being exposed from that side. Still, he was not supposed to entertain the journalist, let alone disclose the details of the truth to him.

All Tägtgren could do now, was to hope that neither

Penny nor her opposition would find out that he showed Sam Cleave the cordoned off site of the Alice detector, there where no-one was supposed to go. All he was supposed to do after Penny told him to speak to Cleave, was to play dumb and keep to the short circuit story, according to the other faction he worked for. But in his fascination and the thrill of knowing what others did not, the first-time spy appeared to have royally fucked himself. He could recover from this heinous mistake only if his revelation remained undetected.

"Look," Albert's superior announced, "look over there, but the storage pod. Do you see what I see?"

Albert's skull started pounding under the torment of a terrible headache. In all honesty he could not see what his boss referred to, which gave him a faintly soothing feeling of sincere innocence. Any ignorance would be true while he could not discern what he was supposed to. "I see nothing out of the ordinary, sir."

"Listen Al, during your shift last night a fully functional capacitor disappeared from the little amount of operational material we still had left after the bloody fire," the man noted angrily. He stared furiously at Albert, waiting for an answer. "Do you know that anything missing on you watch will be charged to you? Worse yet, you might be sited for theft."

"No!" Albert cried inadvertently. "I'm sorry. I just…I am not responsible for this."

"You damn well *are* responsible for it!" his boss sneered.

"No, I mean. I did not steal it. I am not responsible for the theft. I do realize that I must be at fault for allowing it to be taken, indirectly, I suppose," he confessed in disappointment.

"I'm going to have to write a report about this to the company. I will let you know tomorrow what the board decided to do about this," the head engineer sighed. Shaking his head, he walked away, "You are excused for today, Tägtgren. Go home."

"I wish I could. Wish I never left Sweden," he retorted just soft enough not to be heard by the livid supervisor who disappeared among the staff. "That goddamn journalist stole it."

He took the boss' advice and truthfully he was quite relieved about the dismissal for the day. There was too much going on at work that added to his constant anxiety and a break would do him well. In fact, in this angry weather Albert elected to drop in on one of the local bars in Meyrin that was not too far from his apartment. It was his intention to get hammered and forget about his troubles, at least for the day. But not before he called Sam Cleave to pick that bone.

He was met with more disappointment, getting only Sam's voicemail.

"This is Albert Tägtgren, the idiot who foolishly trusted you yesterday. You are a coward, Cleave! You don't even have the balls to pick up the phone, you bastard! I know what you did! And you knew I could not implicate you, because then my employers would know that I told you about the storage container and what I saw there," he shouted on the phone. Albert was livid. "I am going to track you down and we will sort this out, you and I. You can count on that!" He ended the call there and flung his phone on the passenger seat of his car as he neared the checkpoint from his section.

From the perimeter of the compound the Volvo roared, liberated from the security check and leaving behind a myriad of questions, cover-ups and clandestine espionage. Albert finally allowed himself to smile as he looked in his rear view mirror, watching the particle physics laboratory grow smaller in his wake. It felt wonderful, even with the sudden shower of rain that assaulted the area with a posi-tively vicious trajectory that clapped against his wind shield. He winced at the impact, hoping there would not be any impending hail to damage his luxury car before he got to park it under cover.

Thunder shook the ground as the heavy electrical storm system spread out as predicted by the weather bureau. By nightfall torrential havoc would apparently have reached a radius spanning Lyon, Tarare and Villefranche-sur-Saône in neighboring France.

In the near distance two gray figures came into view from the predominantly white environment of mist and showers. They came into view as he slowly drew closer. Two traffic officers were redirecting cars into the detour set up away from the main road.

"Now? In the rain we have to take some shitty pot-hole path?" he grunted, vexed by the extra time he would have to spend on the road. His phone rang. He stopped his car. Was it Sam Cleave?

Albert placed his phone on the hands-free station and answered as he slowly pulled away from the shoulder of the road again. A scratchy sound came across the speaker, then the voice he dreaded most – his other employer, the man who paid him more than Penny did.

"Albert, you told the journalist things you shouldn't have."

"No. No, I told him nothing, sir. Nothing."

"Really? Then what was he doing in the prohibited area with you?" the stern man asked, provoking a renewed panic in Tägtgren. He stopped his car again, barely 200m from the detour sign.

"I don't know what you mean, sir," he swallowed hard.

"CCTV, you blithering idiot!" his employer roared. "For an engineer you are exceedingly stupid! But worse, Albert, you are a *liar.*"

With that the call was cut and the engineer swore he could hear his heart clamoring in his body. His transgression was discovered. It was time to get away, go back home to his country.

Albert decided to turn up the radio to drown out the din of the downpour as he carefully navigated the rather narrow tarmac ribbon he had turned off on toward Meyrin. He reduced speed as he allowed the music to lull his sensibilities and calm his nerves, even when his hands refused to stop shaking.

He looked back to see the unfortunate officers having to stand in the rain and wait for the next cars to direct away. Albert watched the dwindling figures in his rear view mirror. But when the next cars came they had removed the detour sign. The rest of the cars passed on the highway. Completely perplexed the engineer frowned, paying too much attention to what was going on behind him to see what was coming from ahead.

CHAPTER 12

*L*ydia labored away at the programming of the so-called co-ordinates she had created for the experiment. She marked each field and measured the intensity and propulsion from each generator on the grid of the machine. Sam was busy mocking Purdue's getup in the background while she finalized the second stage of the experiment. Healy was on stand-by to do all the heavy lifting – the levers, the multiple vacuum locks and the door, since Sam would be occupied by his filming.

"Purdue, come, let me give you these," Lydia summoned, holding out two small gadgets. "Sam, you may film this is you wish."

"Aye. On it," he replied, following Purdue to record the revelation of what Lydia called '*necessary aids for communication and safe return.*' Sam and Purdue exchanged a look. "But it is just an experiment, right?"

"Yes, Sam," she sighed, "but if it works Purdue will need these to not get lost in the timespace continuum, see?"

"Get lost?" Purdue asked.

"Think of these two devices as the physics counterpart of

a floatation kit, gentlemen," Lydia explained. "This is a communication device of sorts, should you need to contact me from wherever you are."

"Or *whenever* you are," Sam chipped through his almost pursed lips.

"You're so funny," Purdue remarked, looking slightly worried at last. He saw how meticulously she handled the experiment, almost as if she had done it a hundred times before. With this level of dedication she must have been under the impression that her theory was actually plausible in a practical sense.

"This is called the BAT," she announced.

"An abbreviation?" Sam asked.

"No, it uses luminiferous ether like a bat uses echolocation. It will allow you to leave a message in the ether, but you only have thirty seconds of every twenty four hours to do so, provided you have access to chronology, of course," she described to Purdue, occasionally looking straight at Sam's lens as if she wanted it recorded as instruction. Lydia gave Purdue the small box, covered in black fabric. "The mic is concealed under the material and the record button is…" she took his thumb in her hands and ran it along the one side until he felt the button, "…there."

"Got it," Purdue affirmed, memorizing where it was.

"Very important," she warned loudly, "once you press that button, Purdue, you have to put the device down or it will dissolve your hand on a cellular level. POOF!"

Sam's eyes left the view finder and he looked at Purdue. The billionaire was ashen, staring back at Sam. They shared an unspoken exclamation of alarm before Purdue frowned at Lydia, "Excuse me?"

"Oh come now, Purdue!" she said, throwing back her head.

"Why the hellish disintegration, for those of us who do

not possess the aptitude for particle freakishness?" Sam jested, but under it he was quite serious.

Lydia was clearly extremely annoyed by their sudden inquisitiveness and doubt in her system. "Sam, this little box has to make a call before Purdue can talk, right?"

"Aye, that I get."

She continued in a deliberately slow manner to patronize the journalist properly. "And to make that call it has to heat up and manipulate the sound waves in the microphone to find their way on a molecular basis...much as the particles you are made up of communicates among a vast network of nerves and cells inside the landscape that is your body. Are you with me so far?"

"Jesus."

"Right," she went on, "so if your molecules are in contact with an object...the little box...that heats up hotter than the sun, you will not have the ability to say shit, will you?"

Purdue's eyes remained frozen in their cases as he glared at the floor in thought.

"She didn't have to be so utterly condescending," Sam mumbled to himself.

"Healy! Bring me that other velvet bag, please," she called.

"Christ, Purdue! Are you sure you want to do this?" Sam whispered, pausing his recording.

"It's unlikely time travel is even practically viable, Sam. Let's just humor her," Purdue shrugged, but Sam persisted in his urgency. "I have a bad feeling about this."

"What if nothing happens?" Purdue played devil's advocate.

"Purdue," Sam whispered, "what if it works?"

"Purdue," Lydia snapped, "we are running out of time. It's almost evening and here we are fucking about all day with petty hold-ups! This is a very important experiment, for God's sake, so let's make it happen."

"And what is that?" Purdue asked quickly, distracting Lydia from a definite brewing tantrum that would soon merit another tirade. He pointed at the bag she held.

"This is your way back," she informed him. "You have only three days before your BAT runs out of power and will not be able to accelerate enough to send you back.

"So the BAT is also my capacitor?" Purdue asked, as Sam once more moved silently around them to record the proceedings.

"Yes, you have at most three 24-hour periods before it loses its juice, each allowing only 30 seconds of communication per 12-hour pop. That gives you *at most* six opportunities to communicate, probably half that, depending on its power. When you have to come back, press the button twice and put the BAT down. Purdue, there is no undo button once you have done that. Trust me. Make sure you are ready to return before you press that button twice."

Her eyes pierced him with urgency and serious caution.

"Now...at the moment you transcend from this point this device here will record your unified fields' references and keep it saved in its data bank," she continued. In her hand she held a delicate item, a pinkish, semi-transparent dental plate fashioned from the roof of Purdue's mouth. "You need to remove this and used the wire that hooks around your two canines to plug it into the BAT before that double-button activation, are you clear on that?"

"My God," Sam whispered.

"What's wrong, Sam?" she asked him.

"I am just...in absolute awe of your planning, your inventions," he exalted her, hitting that welcome zone of narcissism in Lydia. "It blows my mind!"

Purdue smiled at Sam's clever manipulation by means of that familiar charm that stole Nina from Purdue's embrace a few years ago. He had to admire the schoolboy charm of the dark eyes journalist with his stocky athleticism and wild black hair. Inside, Purdue knew full well that Sam's exclamation was in fact one of subdued terror, the type unleashed from a confrontation with unbridled madness.

ON THE WALL clock the long hand reached six and the short arm pointed just short of nine. The weather was slowly growing more restless. Healy came down from the second story and reported, "Madam, there is a severe thunderstorm headed this way within the next few hours, moving over from Switzerland and due in the south of Germany by tomorrow afternoon, they say. I venture to guess it is a rather serious storm for most of Western Europe."

"Thanks Healy. Do you hear that, gentlemen?" Lydia asked.

Purdue shook Sam's hand and gave him a pat on the back, using his nonchalant approach to serious things to show Sam that he had no faith in the potency of this experiment. He stepped into the buzzing environment of the chamber that was now at the threshold between warming up and powering up for the actual initiation of the launch.

Light rain tapped against the windows by now and the wind bent the tree tops outside, but the people in Jenner Manor had no idea, thanks to the boarded up windows and walls keeping out all external sound. It was a dangerous ignorance that would influence their time sensitive experiment. Healy locked Purdue in the chamber as Sam filmed it.

Sam hoped that the experiment would come to nothing but a big ruckus, a jolt or two and a circuit blown on the mother board of the controlling computer before Lydia would realize it was just another failure. Then she would go back to the drawing board with her theories and allow the men to have a fee drinks while they watched the football at a local sports bar. That was Sam's ideal outcome in the cozy safety of his mind.

Lydia looked into the lens, but she was not speaking to Sam. "Voyager III, time travel experiment number 14, 22 June 2015 in Jenner Manor, located in the city of Lyon, France. Subject: Inventor and scientist David Matthew Purdue, aged forty nine and the time is now..." she looked up, "...8.30 in the evening."

She gestured for Sam to follow her to the control board. On the keyboard she punched in a combination code and the schematic from the map-like paper on the table came up on the screen. Color coded numbers in sequence ran upward as the heat index rose outside the chamber to facilitate the acceleration of the unseen particles inside with Purdue.

The weather rumbled, but Lydia heard nothing. Only Healy discerned something with his keen ears aided by the slight cold draft that crept under the door down the hallway. While they did not need him he quietly made his way to the kitchen and the back door to ascertain the authenticity of the sensation.

"Oh my God!" he gasped as he entered the dark kitchen, the only normal room in the entire mansion. The windows clanged with the heavy downpour which had broken out over Lyon in the last fifteen minutes. Under the door the water was spraying in, wetting the tiles. As the butler placed some newspapers in the slit under the door the thunder bellowed, releasing three rapid flashes of lightning before he pulled his hand away in fright. Healy was a tough, steely operative in his day and even now there were few targets that could elude his aim. But one thing nobody knew was that Rupert Healy was terrified of thunder and lightning.

Petrified, but aware that his job could never suffer under his phobias, he slipped away and returned to the lower level of the house where there was life, and safety from the horrendous nature that sought to do him harm. But as Healy turned the corner into the corridor that led to Lydia and her friends he noticed that the lights were flickering profusely. Clearing his throat under the discomfort of the situation Healy progressed down the almost dark passage, certain that he should not share the weather conditions with an already on-edge Lydia.

A leak inside the wall moistened the plating, an honest mistake by Lydia and Healy not to have noticed before. Rains like these were not a common thing and they had no way of knowing that the plating in the chamber room was being compromised. At the height of the ignition the small window to the chamber was illuminated entirely in bright white light. Sam filmed, but his terrified frozen gaze was fixed on the rays that had now eaten up Purdue's silhouette.

But Lydia paid no attention. She turned a huge dial, and old fashioned knob that initiated the sound factor, a pulsing ultrasound wave that sounded like an unborn heart on sonar, only deeper and slower. Lydia's chest heaved with the excitement of her experiment coming to fruition and a crack of a smile started on her face. A mighty clash cracked in a majestic bouquet of sparks from the wall plating and throughout the house the power died instantly.

"Oh, Jesus Christ! No! Oh my God, no!" Healy heard Lydia scream. She was hysterical, going off on a surge of curses as she frantically flicked switches in the dark. "Healy! Do something! Get the circuits running!"

"On it, Madam!" Healy cried as he scuttled for the circuit board.

"What do I do, Lydia?" Sam shouted.

"Just keep filming," she said with an uncontrolled quiver in her voice.

With a jolt the electricity came on, but what they could not hear sealed Purdue's fate. Outside a massive bolt of lightning struck the house, utilizing the reinforced walls to conduct the overloaded current. Its force intensified not only the marked fields but also overloaded the sonic aspect. Healy covered Lydia with his body while Sam fell backward to the floor as the chamber glowed with fire, but as soon as they beheld it, space swallowed it up.

"The fire disappeared into nothing!" Sam screamed, recalling Tägtgren's story vividly.

Panting and terrified Sam and Healy stood helplessly waiting for the chamber to cool down. They had no idea if Purdue was alive. Behind them in the stench of fire and smoke Lydia smiled with relieved satisfaction.

"Sam," she said calmly, "tell me you captured that on film."

CHAPTER 13

*N*ina Gould was home for the first time in months. Her restored home in Oban, Scotland, needed a serious cleaning. Thanks to the superstitious folk of her home town, whereto she had returned two years before with the purchase of said house, few cleaning ladies agreed to keep up the place while she was away. Once or twice a month the forty one year old history lecturer and advisor would fork out some extra dough to bring a cleaning service in from Edinburgh. She also used to hire *McDusty Domestics* from Argylle when she lived in Ediburgh, because she was pedantic about service. This was why she figured they would do nicely for the old property in Oban she almost lost two years ago, hardly two days after she had purchased it.

Yet another clumsy experiment, but then courtesy of another academic, was the reason for the near destruction of her house and it took her months to persuade the town council not to demolish her home. It was after all a historical landmark, even though it had been the focus of much superstition and old fashioned witch hunting since she was a child from another part of town.

"Mrs. Manning, I will pay you double if you and the girls could come tomorrow," Nina said, pacing around barefoot in her jeans. "You know that the house has been quiet since we had the renovators over, so what is the problem?"

Clearly the manager of the cleaning service gave Nina an uphill battle, unwilling to abandon the old reputation of the house. Nina reached for her pack of Marlboros and put the phone on speaker so that she could light one before she lost her temper.

'Dr. Gould, I appreciate your attempts to fix that place, but we simply do not want to come in there. And that is our prerogative, don't you think?' the woman's mature voice explained in a Scots-Gaelic drawl that irritated Nina beyond reason.

"Well, then, can you refer me to someone? Someone who is not going to charge me too much," Nina muttered around the fag between her lips, sucking on it for just a morsel of relief from the frustration. "My house is too big for me alone to clean."

'I'll see what I can do, dear. Will pass around your number, alright? I'm so sorry,' Mrs. Manning lamented.

"Aye, I'm sure you're real fucking sorry," Nina growled after the call disconnected from the other side, surrounding her head with glorious billows of tobacco and tar. "Fucking cowards. Chicken shit bitches," she kept cussing by herself as she went to the kitchen for some wine. Nina caught a glimpse of the trapdoor that peeked out slightly from under the large woven mat. It gave her the chills, the incidents of that day still reminiscent in her recollection, that day that was the genesis of her friend's eventual demise at the hand of the Order of the Black Sun. She used the ball of her foot to push the mat over the trapdoor, hoping that keeping it from her sight would alleviate her from past nightmares.

Other than the trapdoor in the kitchen and the attic's hollowed wall, her house was far from sinister to her. As a matter of fact Nina was quite surprised at how harmoniously she lived here, without incident, no ghosts or strange phenomena as dictated by the house's reputation. Sure, those rumors were once true, but after the big happening in the basement all those months before things changed completely. Purdue helped her fund the renovations, alterations and repairs so that Nina would have a lot to show the town council in defense against their decisions to demolish the place.

Downstairs the wicked well was filled and covered, but she never went down there unless absolutely necessary. As she poured her wine it tainted her thoughts and memories just a little.

'Imagine if something pushed up through that well, Nina. Imagine if they did a half assed job and the cement is cracking as we speak,' her inner voice, one which obviously belonged to a sadist, presented her with impossible possibilities. Nina took a big swig of the wine to put to sleep her rising gloom. Cleaning. Cleaning services. Stubborn old Scottish wenches and cleaning; that was what she would think of. Profusely, at that.

The phone rang suddenly and Nina uttered a little yelp, spilling some of her drink in startled awkwardness.

"Jesus, Mrs. Manning!" she gasped. She grabbed the phone and answered, "Please tell me you got me someone to clean out my attic."

A male voice replied, "Is that a metaphor? I am sure a beautiful woman such as yourself would have no problem finding a cleaner or two."

"Fuck you, Sam," Nina smiled.

"That is what I implied, yes," he retorted. "You do catch on quickly."

Nina shook her head, chuckling at her old boyfriend's

wit. "How have you been? Heard you were covering the CERN incident," she said.

"Well, this is why I am calling, actually. I was wondering if you would care to join me for a while," Sam said, suddenly sounding a bit unsure of himself.

"In Geneva?" she asked, sitting down at the kitchen table.

"Actually, in Lyon. In France. I'm in France for the next... um, indefinitely," he told Nina. She could hear that something was amiss.

"What are you doing there?" she asked, sipping the remaining wine she had no spilled.

"I was helping Purdue..." he started.

"Wait, wait, wait!" she cut him short. "You and Purdue? Again? Sam, you have to stop calling me with 'you and Purdue' matters. I am tired of almost dying."

"This is different," Sam replied, not once denying that she had every right to decline on her grounds.

"How is it in any way different, Sam? If Purdue is involved it is dangerous. If you are involved it is worth exposing. Those two factors pretty much narrows it down to one thing – my life will be in danger!" she moaned, looking for more wine.

Sam knew she was right and with her feisty nature she would have no reservation to hanging up on him. It was no use to convince her that this case was different from the typical excursion they usually ended up on, so he went with humor.

"At least you'll be in great company again."

"Sam."

"This is really something unique, Nina. It is somewhat unbelievable, actually. We really need you for this, otherwise we might never see Purdue again," he explained hesitantly. He did not want to say that, but he knew Purdue being in peril would impress upon Nina the seriousness of the matter. He was correct in his assumption.

"Excuse me? Where is Purdue?" she asked, frowning over the revelation and the lack of wine in her alcohol cabinet.

Sam resisted the temptation to refer to 'where' as 'when' again and promptly answered, "We don't know. We have some idea, but we will need an expert on German history to help us find him."

He was content with the formulation of that statement. It sounded sane enough to make her come without sounding too trivial for her to decline. Sam waited on the other side of the line. Nina could hear the almost inaudible buzz of the active call.

She had to concede that getting a cleaning service for her house this week was futile anyway and that she could do with a bit of company away from the sneers and scowls of Oban's small minded. "Alright. Where are you in Lyon? And Sam, if anyone tries to kill me we never sleep together again."

"Ouch!" he replied.

"I am really done with these treasure hunts," she reiterated.

"I know, love. And I promise you one hundred percent that this is not a treasure hunt in any form," he assured her. "It's a hunt for Purdue."

CHAPTER 14

enny Richards held the handset against her ear, but she said nothing for a long while. Her eyes stared ahead of her, past her desk and her visitor chairs into the black throat of the fireplace on the other side of her office at the Institute.

"Miss Richards," the voice on the phone pressed. "Did you hear what I said?"

"How did it happen?" she asked slowly.

"His Volvo was obliterated by a runaway 16 wheeler on a back road off the highway between CERN and his resident town of Meyrin. The truck driver told the police that his brakes failed him after he was directed onto the particular road by traffic officers. They stood at a detour sign at the junction of the opposite direction from which Albert was coming," the man on the phone said.

"Thank you so much for letting me know, Martin. Did he work with you on the CMS too?" Penny asked, playing the naïve card.

"No, my dear. I tried to get him to work with us after I got his resume from you, but they delegated his skills to the

Alice team. I suppose they needed more expertise than us," he teased.

Penny knew there was an endearing competition between the scientists and engineers of the two detectors since the super Collider's inception. She had contacted Martin West-dijk when the threats started against the Institute, using the premise that Albert Tägtgren was her brother-in-law. With subterfuge she convinced Westdijk and his colleagues that Albert would be the right acquisition for their cause, to facil-itate his infiltration of the laboratory effectively.

"My husband is going to take this very hard," she sighed, sounding positively morose.

"Again, my dear Penny, my sincerest condolences. I told him that very morning to wait for me so that we could have dinner, but he chose to leave in the middle of the day," the old professor complained. "Agh, had he only stayed till I got off he would never have taken that bloody road."

"Oh, Martin, we shouldn't bemoan things we cannot change, especially things that are not our fault," Penny consoled the old man she met years ago when he worked with her husband on a project in the Netherlands. She fondly recollected their late nights in the recreational room, playing billiards and drinking. Not one for particle physics she would just sit and listen to their playful arguments about quantum gravity and Einstein's unified field theory. It was fascinating how much they knew, eventually sounding like inebriated gods challenging the science of Creation. But after the end of the project their roads just drifted apart over the years to come; that was, until Penny needed a favor from Professor Westdijk to get Albert into CERN. If he only knew what the Swedish engineer was really doing there.

"Well, Martin, thank you again for giving me the real story. I don't trust the media or the police with the truth, as you know," she said, lighting one of her long, slender cigarettes.

"You are welcome. I know. Your family deserved to hear it from a friend, not some bloody investigator or reporter. I bid you adieu, my dear Penny. We'll speak soon once I have some time off to catch up, yes?" Professor Westdijk said.

"That'd be lovely, Martin. My love to Gerda."

Penny sat bewildered, resting her chin on folded hands as she leaned on her elbows. It was too uncanny that her spy ended up dead right after he spoke to the media, after he spoke to Sam Cleave. Her heart raced with rage. Sam Cleave had betrayed her trust. It was not the first time he was associated with questionable organizations. Reputedly he was a member of the Brigade Apostate, a clandestine order of scientists, soldiers, historians and moguls – in fact, influential men and women the highest of their respective disciplines and vocation. She did not know what they stood for, really, but any club that recruits so many brilliant people in so wide a spectrum globally was to be wary of, she thought.

Penny picked up the phone. "Caitlin, please get Foster to come and see me. Thank you."

CHRISTIAN FOSTER WAS a free agent – quite literally. He worked for the Cornwall Institute on many occasions before but respectfully declined becoming a permanent fixture in their security arena. He worked by contract only and strictly adhered to specific rules. Sometimes he would even take on assassination jobs, but they left a bad taste in his moral mouth. Christian was just what his name implied. His God-fearing ways made him very trustworthy, but for those organizations who needed a little chilli with their serving of punishment, he was not the best chef. He loathed unnecessary violence.

"Christian, so good of you to come," Penny nodded as the man she summoned knocked on the open door of her office.

"Good afternoon, Miss Richards. How are you?" he smiled.

"I'm not too well, I'm afraid. That is why I need to discuss something with you," she said cordially. "Please, sit."

"That is the downside of my reputation, regrettably," he replied as he sat down opposite her at her desk.

"What is that?" she asked, gesturing to her assistant outside the doorway.

"My name only comes up when something unpleasant is afoot," he lamented. "It would have been nice to be called to rescue someone for a change."

Penny looked at the very attractive Nordic looking man. He was remarkable on so many levels, even more by his dress sense. "Well, Christian, I never find it unpleasant to be paid a visit by you, if that is any consolation," she flirted lightly.

"It is quite the reprieve for me, yes, for what I am usually summoned for," he chuckled. "What is on your mind, Miss Richards?"

Penny sighed. She took the time to look at his exceptionally tall and powerful frame, clothed in all black. Around his neck hung a diamond Christian cross, the crusts of the pristine gem embedded in silver or steel, the difference of which was indiscernible to Penny's untrained eye. Nevertheless it was beautiful against the black background of his Oriental shirt.

"We hired a journalist to do a harmless interview for us. Now the man he interviewed has perished under suspicious circumstances and the journalist has disappeared. But he vanished after being seen on a security monitor trespassing in a section of CERN he had no permission for, Christian," she informed him, feeling uncomfortable under his narrow grey eyes. "He was seen recording footage of something rather valuable to this institute, something that needed to remain undiscovered," she explained.

Christian's gaze tore from Penny. He looked up at the ceiling, mulling the information over. Christian Foster's ash blond hair fell to his chest, looking even lighter against his dark clothing. Penny admired his angelic semblance.

'If he were an angel, I bet he'd be Michael,' she thought, just before his face sank back to lock eyes with her.

"Do you have a credit card trail, something to steer me to a point of origin from where I might track him? I doubt the nuclear laboratory in Switzerland would have any trace of him that they would be willing to share with me?" he asked Penny.

"Actually, Christian, that was precisely the route I was going to suggest you employ to start you on your way. Would that be too difficult for you?" she asked innocently, masking her reverse psychology with a tone of accommodation.

"No, it is doable, Miss Richards. I was just hoping not to have to resort to guile to obtain my information," he shrugged with a smile. "Besides, it would take a great deal more time than to just find a last stay or purchase to locate him."

"I understand. That was my thought exactly. The problem is that my hackers and investigating staff could not find any evidence of card activity or cell phone communication since Sam Cleave disappeared," she said.

"Perhaps he was killed as well," Christian suggested.

"That also crossed my mind, especially since he had gathered an immense amount of detail about our covert operation. Still, I need to find him, dead or alive, just to make sure what hand he is holding in this very sensitive gamble," Penny explained.

"I see," Christian Foster yielded finally. "Let me get my

paperwork to your secretary in an hour and as soon as I received payment accordingly, I shall commence my search."

He rose from his chair and straightened his clothing, towering over her. Penny shook his hand, always her favorite part of meeting with him, "Be in touch, Christian. You expertise is invaluable in this matter and we will be grateful for your swift and urgent attention."

"I shall give it my utmost attention, Miss Richards. Penny," he smiled, leaving Penny weak in the knees at the mention of her first name.

"Good bye," she chimed as he withdrew his hand.

"God bless," he said simply and with a gentlemanly nod he turned and left.

Penny Richards gasped, fanning her face with the folder in her hand as she watched him walk away, "Jesus Christ, that man is hot!"

CHAPTER 15

*P*urdue woke with a headache just short of a nuclear meltdown. It was so intense that his eyeballs felt swollen, pushed from their holes by a swollen, pulsing brain. In fact, his jaw throbbed with what felt to him like the aches he used to endure suffering the flu – a dull pain that ran through the substance of his facial muscle. But for all their battling to function he found his eyes to be absolutely useless. No matter how he stretched his lids, no matter where he looked about him, darkness the density of rock harbored his burning hot body.

Fever possessed Purdue's entire physique; so much so, that he felt that his lips had gone numb and tingly. Blisters had formed on the edges of his mouth and his skin felt like the time he spent too much time in the pool during the 1982 Outback heat wave with his Australian girlfriend's family. Barely unable to move from the muscle aches and the scalded skin, Purdue found himself moaning like a weak boy after a hernia operation. His head was spinning. In truth Purdue had no idea if he was dead or alive.

"Help!" he shouted inadvertently, expecting a hollow echo

that reached through eternity, but the one word escaping his painful lips bounced back to him in the near distance. He reckoned by the travel of sound that he was in a room, one that was not small, but it was definitely not a hall or cavern.

'Maybe you should not call out, old boy,' his common sense told him. *'You have no idea who is listening.'* Under him he could feel cold concrete and some loose mortar that must have fallen from a wall, but he was too afraid to reach out to his sides. Who knew what he might push his hands into! Besides, since he was convinced that this was death, specifically some hellish destination by point of his suffering, whatever sat next to him could be nothing good.

With immense ardor Purdue changed position onto his knees. It was excruciating and he moaned as quietly as he could. Under his palm tiny stones stung his sore hands. He grasped one of them and lobbed it into the dead blackness in front of him.

It landed not far from him with a blunt clap.

His heart raced at the prospect of what would transpire here in a place that could harbor anything his imagination could conjure. Things capable of unnatural acts, things of unfathomable abilities could very well come at him from the dense nothingness around him and here he was throwing rocks at it.

All these crazy things crossed Purdue's pounding mind, but he had to find out where he was regardless. There was no use in remaining stagnant, static in fear for an eternity. Boredom and unsatisfied curiosity would present utter torment if he allowed his innate wariness to drown his courage. He had to keep moving, gathering information. The stone he flung had made a sound that resembled dropping pebbles on a cobblestone road. If his ears did not deceive him the rock had struck a stone wall or object. When he crawled forward the wrenching sting of a dislocated knee ruptured his leg at the bend. Purdue screamed blue murder from the unbearable pain, falling on his stomach and just lay there panting to find his senses. Delirious with pain, he hoped that he did not alert the wrong attention to his presence. Yet no sooner had he thought that…

"Please don't find me," he whispered as the footsteps approached from somewhere in the dark. Purdue tried desperately for his grinding teeth not to make a sound while the pain slowly overwhelmed his ability to contain it. But he had to be quiet. From nearby he discerned the language of the male voices as being German.

"Oh God, no," Purdue whispered into the dust under his sheltered face as he lay with his forehead on his folded arms. He smelled moist mossy residue on the ground. Once his skin adapted to the pain as much as it could while his nerve endings screamed, Purdue looked up to see if there was any way he could tell where he was. Hearing the distinct German conversation filled his heart with gloom, but he did not know why. All he knew was that he did not speak the language apart from the well known 'please' and 'thank you' most people had a command of.

Slightly above his brow, a few meters in front of him a small white line ran horizontally from left to right. It was impossible for the bewildered billionaire to figure out what it was at first. But when darting black shadows moved behind it Purdue realized that the white line he was so fascinated by was in fact a crack under a door, letting light through.

"At least I'm not dead," he sighed as he inched his sore body forward. The doors opened and there stood two lean figures in German uniforms. "But I am definitely in hell."

Purdue's head sank back into the safety of his folded arms as he heard the two men shouting for medics. That much he could translate. He expected to be severely beaten, or just shot in the head, but within a short while two young military medics brought a stretcher and lifted Purdue onto it with great care. They kept telling him to relax, to try to breathe deeply, but he did not understand their suggestions.

The two officers who discovered Purdue in the basement of the Reich Chancellery accompanied him to the infirmary. From his befuddled expression at their questions they quickly realized that he was not one of them.

"Sprechen sie Deutsch?" one asked. It was a phrase Purdue was familiar with, but he knew full well that the entire language eluded his abilities and if he attempted to feign comprehension it would take no longer than a minute to discover that he was no German.

"Nein, leider nicht," he replied through his pained expression, doing his best to sound as educated in their tongue as he could.

"I like that," the one officer smiled at the other. "He knows how to say in German that he does not speak German."

The other one chuckled, lighting a cigarette and leaning hard on Purdue's scalded body. His face came so close that Purdue could smell his foul breath.

"They probably teach the Allied soldiers that in case they get captured," the other said, speaking to his colleague but addressing Purdue. "What is your name, soldier?"

"I am not a soldier. My name is David Purdue," Purdue groaned, his skin burning under the pressure of the officer's spiteful leaning.

"And what country are you from, David?" the other officer asked.

"Scotland. I'm from Scotland, but I am not a soldier," he insisted. However, with every attempt at denying his capacity the aggressive officer would press a little harder on Purdue's sore body, reveling in the stranger's screams.

"Sturmbannführer Gestern, what is the protocol for

Allied spies captured in the Führer's bomb shelter?" the vile tormentor asked the seated, smoking officer on the other side of Purdue's bed.

"I think…" Gestern mocked, looking up in thought, "… dismemberment? No, no, I think drowning."

"Wait, I am in Hitler's bunker?" Purdue asked, shocked. For his common use of their leader's name he received a deafening clout against the head that sent his brain into a jolt of pain.

"You are in the Reichskanzlei in Wilhelmstraße, imbecile! You infiltrated the Führer's seat without being detected and then you want to play dumb and pretend that you don't know where you are?" Gestern shouted at Purdue, ripping from his torso what was left of his flame tattered shirt. Purdue screamed as the fabric peeled away some of the skin it had melted into during his voyage combustion.

"Gestern! Haupt!" Purdue heard a woman's voice call to the two officers on the other side of the curtain that was drawn around his bed in the infirmary. They jumped up, erect and serious. It was obvious that the woman merited their utmost respect. A brief conversation ensued between the three of them before the curtain was drawn away and there stood the most beautiful woman Dave Purdue had ever beheld.

"Hello," she said, surveying Purdue's wounds without touching him. In silence she shook her head. Then she requested the two officers leave the infirmary, but they reminded her that they were responsible for the prisoner until he was interrogated and Himmler decided what to do with him. The mere fact that he entered a virtually impenetrable bunker without detection made him a special point of interest to the SS.

Maria allowed them to remain, on the condition that they keep quiet until she had dressed the prisoner's wounds and cleaned him up. "They are waiting outside. Your name is?" she asked as she ran water into a large bowl to wash Purdue's wounds.

"David Purdue," he groaned, overwhelmed by the shooting pain of damaged nerve endings. In his mouth his tongue probed at something unnatural. The roof of his mouth had a plate fixed perfectly to it, molded to its unique curvature.

"I am Maria," she smiled. He could not stop staring at the beautiful blond woman. Her hair was extremely long, tied into a horse tail that swayed on her buttocks as she moved. Full lips and large light blue eyes adorned her perfect facial features like well set gems, although he could see she was no child anymore. Purdue guessed the stunning creature in her forties, perhaps, but with the ethereal perfection of her appearance her age did not even factor.

"How did you get into the Reichkanzlei, David?" she asked, gently removing what was left of his shirt until Purdue was naked from the waist up. "It is an impossible thing to accomplish."

"Nothing is impossible, dear Maria," he answered, trying to utilize what charm he could to impress at least one of them here behind enemy lines. But he also needed to maintain a charade of power, so he elected to fib about his vulnerability. He knew the two officers were listening and that his subterfuge could prove helpful in distracting them while he found a way out. "I am not the only one who managed to infiltrate the bunker. Most of my unit came with me."

She tilted her head, ceasing her gentle sponging of his chest. Her striking eyes drilled into his, evoking more than lust in him. Gradually the impending feeling of psychic violation overcame him until he closed his eyes and kept them shut. *'Did she really just read my mind?'* Gestern and Haupt reacted to his revelation, rapidly discussing what to do about the others they had to locate, but Maria did not seem to find the information threatening.

Continuing her cleansing routine she told Purdue, "I am going to fetch you some clean pants and socks. It seems only certain parts of you burned when you…" she studied his eyes again, frowning, "…came here. Just a moment. I'll be back soon." Then she whispered, "I know you are here alone."

Sturmbannführer Haupt rushed to Purdue's side, "How many? How many in you unit?"

Purdue had to think fast. "Only five."

"Fünf andere!" the officer shouted to his colleague, who promptly started barking orders to an unseen company in the next room. The sound of stomping boots passed the infirmary in both directions, accompanied by several order issues.

With Maria out of the room and the officers off on a wild goose chase pursuing what they would never find, Purdue tried to move. His wrists were secured to the steel rods that lined the length of the bed by cuffs, but the rest of his scalded body was free to move. There was very little room to move effectively and the sensation of his raw burned back and arms pulling free of the linen was too much to bear. Purdue felt faint from the intensity of the agony and his head fell back on the pillow. He gasped, trying to control his breathing.

Maria came back, talking to another woman in hushed tones.

"David, this is my friend, Sigrun," Maria announced. Purdue looked up at the equally breathtaking woman to her side and his heart jolted. Shocked and ignorant of the pain Purdue sat upright and in disbelief he started at the dark haired woman.

"Nina?"

CHAPTER 16

Sam's eyes flashed between all the passengers stepping off the train, trying to find Nina among them. It had been two days since she agreed to come to Lyon to help him and Lydia look for Purdue, yet she had no idea of the true absurdity that awaited her. All he wanted was to get her here first, otherwise she would never have agreed to indulge the insane actions Purdue and Sam had perpetrated.

"Are you sure she would be able to help, Mr. Cleave?" Healy asked. He was tasked to accompany the lone journalist whose footage and gear was confiscated by order of Professor Jenner. Lydia was worried that Sam would use the obscure proof of her experimental success to make himself rich and famous, among other threats she assumed would come from the award-winning journalist's recording of her quantum mechanical voyage.

Healy had to come with Sam to prevent him from leaving the country, yet Lydia insisted that Sam Cleave was not a hostage by any means.

"If anyone can help us pinpoint where Purdue is in history, Healy, it is Dr. Nina Gould. She is an expert on

German modern history, especially the Second World War," Sam promised. They both waited at International Arrivals, scanning the crowd that had just come in from Heathrow via Quantas.

"What does she look like, sir?" Healy asked.

Sam smiled. "She is small, but passionate. Nina towers at about 5'3" with a seven foot attitude, dark shoulder length hair with big black eyes like hellfire."

"Sounds like a handful," Healy remarked, provoking Sam to have a laugh at the accuracy of the butler's guess.

"You have no idea. If you think Professor Jenner is rambunctious you have not seen Nina at the height of an idea she is pursuing. Good God, there is no stopping that woman. She is stubborn, smart and articulate."

Healy smiled in the only wry way he knew how. With a nod he added, "How long have you been in love with her, sir?" Sam glared at Healy. He kept silent, studying any sign of the butler's jest, but the tall man was quite sincere.

"Since the moment I met her, Healy. And you will too."

"I will not stand for this, Mr. Lamont! I don't care if you cough up a ball of fur, you will stay here until your staff have located and brought my missing laptop. It is in a black EVA brand laptop case with strap and the zipper is fitted with a tiny, teensy combination lock about the size of your brain!"

"I hear Nina," Sam frowned, rotating to see where her voice came from.

"Could that be the doctor over there, threatening that man?" Healy asked innocently, pointing to an information desk where three agitated employees of the airline bustled to locate a missing bag. By the desk stood the stunning, small historian. Her hair was tied back in a high ponytail and she was dressed smart casually, her shades roughly fixed on her head. Her leather jacket hugged her shapely form and her black jeans fitted her snugly right down to the slightly heeled brown boots she wore, the same color as her luggage bag.

"That's her," Sam grinned. "Are you in love yet?"

He headed to Nina and Healy followed in his trail, answering him, "Yes, sir, but with some form of caution."

Sam laughed. When Nina saw him she blessed him with a lovely smile and opened her arms to receive him in a warm reunion.

"What's this? Old age?" she joked, grabbing Sam by his newly grown groomed beard and moustache which only gave him a more rugged handsomeness.

"Aye, the years are piling on, but I'm going down swingin', lassie," he winked as he gently tugged at the salt and pepper facial hair of the eternally youthful journalist. They embraced tightly, remaining so for almost a minute. Healy could see that Cleave and Dr. Gould had a history, and by the looks of it, a very close one.

"Mr. Cleave, we must make haste before the storm floods the roads home," Healy reminded Sam.

"Oh yes, you're right," Sam agreed, just as the ground operator brought Nina her laptop bag with the small steel lock on the zipper.

"So sorry for the inconvenience, Dr. Gould," she apologized. "We found in two seats down from you, among someone else's luggage."

The weather only grew worse out in the parking area. From all directions the rain pelted the cars and buildings, changing with the switch of the wind direction every few minutes. As Sam directed a cowering Nina by means of a soft hand on her lower back with Healy in their wake, bearing her luggage bags, they raced to get to the car. He could see that the normally stout butler was terrified of the thunder and literally dipped every time there was lightning above. As the wild eyed Healy and Nina scuttled into the vehicle Sam looked up at the terrifying blue veins that developed across the sky in a split second every time the clouds pulsed with light.

His dark eyes reflected the awesome blue-white cracks as he braved the danger to behold the super electrical charge of the majestic lightning. Deep inside Sam he knew this god-like expulsion into the atmosphere was the secret to bringing back Dave Purdue, but he was not prepared to stand there too long and run the risk of its wrath. There would be plenty of time for that, once he persuaded Lydia that the very lightning of the next two days were the key to returning Purdue to her chamber, hopefully unscathed.

They drove to Jenner Manor in the terrible chaos of traffic under the escalating storm while Sam filled Nina in on what had happened during the experiment and why they need a historian to guide Purdue onto the necessary points in history so that they could eventually pin-point him to bring him back to 2015.

"I don't know what to say, Sam. Look, I have a very open mind. You know that. But time travel? Really?" she scowled, believing that Sam believed every word he told her. "I have seen a lot of weird shit that defied explanation before..."

"So why is this so hard to believe, Nina?" Sam asked.

"It's Science Fiction!" she defended.

"And yet here we were, watching Purdue vanish into a flash of fire without a grain of ash to show for his presence!" he retorted. "If he just combusted, or God forbid burned to death, we would have found his remains in the chamber, would we not?"

"It is just..." she hesitated, "...it's just so unreal. It is unlikely. Look, I am not an authority on quantum physics..."

"But Prof. Jenner is, Madam," Healy chipped in from the driver's seat. "I promise you, Dr. Gould, this far-fetched mania is every bit as real as you or I sitting in this car right now. It is only Science Fiction while it remains to be proven. And that is precisely what we have just achieved with the help of Mr. Purdue."

Nina had nothing to throw at the well groomed butler. She had to concede to having seen stranger things than simple quantum dynamics at play. As long as she did not have to run for her life this time, Nina Gould was willing to accept anything Sam and his new consorts dealt her.

When they arrived at the manor an hour and a half later, she saw why Sam was so convinced that the environment could actually facilitate tine travel. Her eyes marveled at the strange sheeting on the fences and the lonely mansion being laid out for protection instead of esthetics.

"Listen, is the lady of the house still going to be awake?" Nina asked as they pulled into the yard. "The windows are dark and there is no indication of life. Won't we wake her?"

"The windows always look like this, Dr. Gould," Healy explained. "It looks like this as a result of the windows being boarded up. Besides, Professor Jenner is somewhat..." he hesitated and smiled at Nina, "...eccentric. Not fond of sleep. She says she'll get plenty of that when she is dead."

"I like her already," Nina smiled, staring out the slowing car's window at the wild garden, lit with bright lights situated around the shutters of the manor. It crossed her mind that it was curious how a woman of such financial means would not bother to beautify what is clearly a stately property with so much potential to be resurrected to its former glory. To Nina Lydia Jenner sounded like someone who took pride only in her work and left the rest to the devil.

When they entered the enormous house, properly wet from the downpour Nina instantly detected the smell of burnt wiring and cannabis, but she did not make mention of it.

"Welcome to the Jenner Manor, madam," Healy smiled as

he brought Nina a thick towel to dry her hair. He had one each for Sam and himself as well. "I shall start a fire in the drawing room."

"Shouldn't you let the professor know we are here?" Nina asked.

Sam chuckled alongside Healy who answered, "I assure you, Dr. Gould, she can hear us."

After Sam took over the hearthing duties from the butler, Healy took to task getting Dr. Gould settled in first. "Dr. Gould, please, let me show you to your room," he invited, taking her bags from her and leading the way up the stairs to the right on the first floor. It was probably the only part of the house that resembled a house and not some under-ground gathering place for mad artists and obscene electricians.

"I hope this is adequate. I did not expect another visitor, so today was a bit of a rush to get some fresh linen. But I gave the room a good grooming," he explained politely.

"And even got fresh roses!" Nina pointed, pleasantly surprised. "I feel special, Healy. There are no other fresh bouquets that I could see in the house."

"That is quite correct, doctor," he agreed. "Normally I would not go to such reaches, but the scent of the flowers and their beauty was a prerequisite for your room. Any lady guest should have roses. For some reason, you complete the bouquet."

'Was he just flirting with me?' she wondered, but felt by no means uncomfortable for it. Healy was not a bad looking bloke at all.

"Well, well," Lydia cried from her wheelchair in the door-way, "it looks like this house has suddenly come alive!"

"Professor Jenner, this is Mr. Cleave's friend, Dr. Nina Gould," Healy announced as he hung Nina's coat on the stand next to her bed.

"I'm sorry to impose like this, but I heard that our mutual friend was in a bind?" Nina told Lydia.

"I'm afraid so. So many years I have devised this plan, created the schematics, built the contraptions all to prove that Nikola Tesla had some very good theories. And with one half-assed attempt at collecting scientific information the goddamn thing decides to work!" Lydia rambled in her hoarse low voice that completely contrasted her attractive, dainty face.

"So you did not mean to send Purdue back in time, then?" Nina marveled.

"I don't know what I expected, Nina. But whatever I tried to prove, inadvertently proved itself. I had never been this collectively disappointed and elated with an experiment's outcome," Lydia sighed. "I mean, the bloody thing worked! Who would have guessed the ludicrous was a matter of mathematics?"

"Not me, for sure," Nina remarked. "I always thought the absurd was the burden of the bard, not the wizard."

Lydia stopped he wheelchair and stared at Nina. Mute, she just looked the historian straight in the eye. Nina felt awkward for her uttering, thinking she may have offended the professor. Lydia suddenly became animate again, lolling her head to one side and extending her fingers like a cat, stretching, "You are a remarkable little thing, Dr. Gould. Such eloquence! I always wished I could wield poetry and philosophy like that, but alas I am not so inclined. I envy you. All I know is locked in numbers and equations with not a hope of ever stringing words as I do compounds."

"For what it is worth, I am dreadfully inept at mathematical problems and anything related to physics. I suppose that is the reason for the differing abilities in people. One has to complete the other, each being an extension of the previous to cover the entire spectrum of all things," Nina said as they neared the warm glow in the drawing room.

"There is that philosophy again," Lydia noted, smiling. "So tell me, Nina, how much do you know about World War II?"

Sam laughed heartily, "She knows enough to have been there, Lydia."

Lydia raised an eyebrow. "Perhaps we should send Nina back the same way to go and get Dave. Nobody would know better how to track down a spoiled adventurer from the present like someone who knows the ways of that era like the back of her hand."

CHAPTER 17

"*G*ood morning. I am here as substitute structural engineer for the Alice," Christian Foster said in a heavy accent nobody he spoke to could place. He made certain that his pronunciation sounded exotic without prompting Swedes or Dutch staff, for instance, to assume he was their fellow countryman. It was all part of his deception.

"Let me contact one of the heads at Atlas, sir. One moment," the pleasant receptionist replied in a very professional manner.

"Uh, no, no," Foster protested, "not Atlas. I am due at the Alice."

She rolled her eyes and shrugged coyly, "I'm so sorry, Mister…" and she stole a look at his security card, "…Millerson. I must have heard you wrong," she smiled. "Forgive me, I am still getting used to all the different accents."

"Please, don't feel bad about it. I am a bit of an acquired taste," he winked.

The receptionist sorted out his appointment and paged the head of the Alice project to meet the new engineer at the cafeteria. "Just over there, Mr. Millerson," she directed him to the clean windows in the aluminum door frames. "Dr. Blake will meet you in the next few minutes."

"Thank you kindly," he dipped his head respectfully, blond tresses tied back and spectacled like a proper science expert. The towering gentleman strode slowly through the milling people. Behind his back the receptionist whispered to a filing clerk, "Fucking hell, Janet, he is delicious!"

"DR. BLAKE, very good to meet you," Foster smiled and shook the hand of the Alice commander. Dr. Blake had already received Foster's credentials, excellently faked beyond his detection and his assistant had already run the mandatory background checks on the falsified identity of the methodical operative.

"Mr. Millerson, it is a pleasure to finally make your acquaintance," Dr. Blake said rather abruptly. He was a man who valued progress and efficiency far above humor or amity, therefore he cut straight to the chase, escorting Foster to what the head of Alice thought was the engineer's new assignment.

As he described the work and presented Foster with all the rules and shifts of the job, Foster's photographic memory recorded the various turns and beacons so that he could find his way if he had to return at some point. No amount of information was ever too trivial for him, and any detail left unused was simply tucked back into his memory. Even as the brilliant mercenary took note of the buildings and the directions of all the detectors inside the 27km pipeline of the Large Hadron Collider, he still took in the wealth of nonsense Dr. Blake was describing. Foster's mind was trained to sift through facts and only keep that which would be beneficial to his mission. Until now there was nothing worth keeping from all the unnecessary facts presented, but then Dr. Blake said something of interest.

"And then they saw him on the closed circuit television, the security people. That is how we found out he was involved in something underhanded. I hope you don't show that much interest in the project, Millerson. Just do your job," Dr. Blake said sternly.

"And after that he was dead?" Foster asked.

"Yes, after he dragged that journalist in here against policy," Dr. Blake replied.

"To do what?" Foster asked in an amazed tone. It was all part of playing innocent, sounding oblivious to the weight of the issue. "I can't believe the lengths to which some people will go for attention."

"Exactly what I thought," Blake agreed, loosening up a bit in the company of such an astute employee. "Sam Cleave was seen just a few minutes later in the company of two strangers right here, non-staff, just like him!"

"Dr. Blake, I think can help with this investigation," Foster urged. "I'm a former police detective. Could I have a quick gander at those two men who accompanied Cleave? It won't take a moment of your time and besides, my shift only starts in twenty minutes."

After much inner deliberation Dr. Blake agreed to take Foster to the security section to run the now infamous clip of the only employee of the CERN LHC project to ever be killed on the job, so to speak. He introduced Foster to the security staff and briefly explained why he would like Foster to have access to the clip. However, Blake had to get back to the Alice and decided to leave Foster with them until the new engineer was due at the detector for his first shift.

"Almost there, let me just shift the timer," one of the security officers told Foster.

"Take your time, by all means," the friendly giant smiled.

"Here it is," the officer said two minutes later. "I'll slow it down for you. You see, we could only catch their movements on the far left of the container. Our interior cameras were destroyed with the initial fire, so we had these temporaries mounted. Not a great view from them, but you can see one of the other men as well as the journalist when they move out from this point here." With his index finger pressed on the screen he marked the area where Foster attention was needed. "Ready?" Foster nodded. The officer played the clip where Sam stalked the two obscured figures at the container, but they were off screen. When Sam stepped through the archway Purdue and Lydia's butler appeared to block off what they construed as an intruder on their intrusion.

"Stop!" Foster shouted, startling the whole office into silence. "Zoom this section in. Can you?"

"Certainly can," the officer said, enlarging the men on the screen.

Foster leaned in and his mouth fell open. Inaudibly he said, "Healy!"

CHAPTER 18

"*N*ina?" Maria laughed. "You will feel better after you have had some sleep, David."

The two beauties giggled over Purdue's strange exclamation. "Is Nina your wife, David Purdue?" Maria smiled as she dressed his wounds very carefully.

"No," he replied with great difficulty through the bolts of pain shooting through his skin wherever the warm sponge touched him. He looked at Sigrun in disbelief. Her eyes, her mouth, the shape of her nose and even her mannerism was that of Nina Gould. While she watched Maria tend to his injuries his eyes constantly met hers and Sigrun's glare would penetrate his mind.

"Nina?" he whispered very softly as Maria's chores whipped up a proper noise when she rinsed the bowls and ran the water. Still Sigrun did not break their visual bond. Purdue looked to see that Maria's back was still turned. "Nina, is that you? Did you come to bring me back?" Sigrun seemed to understand his plight, but not once did she answer him in thought or word.

"Where are your men, soldier?" shouted Sturmbannführer Haupt as he breached the closed door and stormed at Purdue, bayonet in hand.

"You cannot come in here and attack our captives!" Maria reprimanded him. Haupt relented, keeping the point of his blade to Purdue's throat. He stood aside, but remained adamant.

"I am standing right here until you are done with your pampering, Maria. Then the Allied soldier is ours to interrogate.

"So you are going to make a mess of all my good work here?" she snarled. He only shrugged.

Purdue only caught one or two words here and there. He wished he paid more attention when he and Nina had that holiday in Austria a few years ago. But Nina did all the talking there and he did not bother to learn German because she was always there. He looked at the dark beauty of Sigrun, the way in which her long brown ponytail meandered over the curves of her body. Even now, Nina was here, Purdue thought. She was always there.

Sturmbannführer Gestern came in, enquiring when Maria would be done with him. She tried to stall, but to no avail. Purdue's wounds were dressed. Now that his second degree wounds were treated, he would be taken.

"Where are you taking him? I need to redress his wounds every day otherwise the flesh will get septic. He'll get a high fever and then he will die, Gestern," she reminded them.

"We are taking him to a cell right here in the basement of the Reichkanzlei, Maria. There is no sign of his men, so we need to contain them in here until we have flushed them all out," he told Maria.

For the first time in a long while the mysterious dark woman spoke, "Hermann, there are no others."

The German officers were struck mute by her statement. For a moment they just looked at Sigrun, exchanging glances

PRESTON WILLIAM CHILD

between one another and then they scrutinized Purdue's expression. Their Scottish prisoner shrugged, revealing that he had lied to them. Gestern walloped Purdue with a leather gloved fist that cracked two of his teeth.

Against the roof of Purdue's mouth a slight click alarmed him. He could not remember what the thing was or why he had it in his mouth, but something about it was apparently important, as far as his instincts warned.

"You lied to us?" Haupt sneered.

"I had to. You would never believe that I came here on my own," Purdue defended with as cordial a tone as he could. His torso pulsed with agony from the nerve damage. "I will tell you anything you want to know if you just let me get some clothes on." The two officers were reeling to kill the captive, but they were not allowed to just yet. "Bitte?" Purdue tried.

"Stop trying to speak our language, traitor. You are just violating it with your filthy tongue," Haupt commanded. "One more word in German and I will cut out your tongue, yes?"

"Aye," Purdue replied proudly, evoking a fit of laughter from the two men, who continued to make a mockery of him in German to the girls.

"Have you looked up his kilt yet, Maria?" Gestern laughed. Haupt chuckled, leaning on Purdue's shoulder to see his face twist in pain. Maria maintained her English for Purdue's sake.

"Get lost, you two. You are not going to get far with him before Adolf had spoken to him. Now wait outside, so that I can dress him in proper clothes before you take him to the cells," she told them, and they stood right outside, still laughing about the Scotsman and the change of pants.

"Adolf? Purdue groaned. He was terrified at the prospect of what would befall him now, but to speak to Adolf Hitler

118

would be a tarnished honor indeed. "Am I going to speak to Hitler himself?"

"No, my dear David. Adolf Diekmann. And although he is not the Führer, he is in command of the Waffen SS regiment called *'Der Führer'*. It is a coincidence, ja?" Maria told him. Purdue looked at Sigrun. She did not want to depress him even more but thought to alert him. "You would have maybe had a better chance at surviving had you spoken to our Führer instead of Diekmann. He is a monster."

"Oh Christ, if a Nazi calls someone a monster I am as good as dead. And all this before I have even seen Helmut," Purdue moaned to himself.

"Helmut?" Maria asked as she pulled down Purdue's hacked up, charred pants. He desperately wanted to distract the ladies from his manhood, which was about to betray his attraction to them. He spoke loudly to draw their eyes away, "Helmut Kämpfe. I need to see him before I go."

The women stared at one another. "You have business with a German officer of the Waffen SS? How? David, where do you come from?" Maria asked again.

"Scotland," he answered as he felt the hard fabric of new canvas trousers swallow his legs. "Maria, I just need my black flint box, please. It is in my pocket there. And my little note pad. I am a bit of a poet and like to make notes."

She obliged, placing the BAT in Purdue's pocket along with the small pad, which was down to about four pages before expiry and not worth perusing.

"Sigrun?" Maria exclaimed suddenly.

"Nina?" Purdue persisted.

Sigrun sat staring at Purdue, her hands clawing at her thighs as if she was having a fit.

"You are not from this realm. You are not from this realm. David Purdue knows the future. David Purdue is an oracle who will tell us the future but he will not change it. He will not change the thread..." Sigrun rambled in a monotone voice that came in one long trance-like growl.

"Why do you keep calling her Nina?" Maria asked fearfully. "Who are you really?"

"You will never believe me. But I think she is my former lover, one of my friends who came back to help me escape!" Purdue frantically gripped at Maria's collar, whispering hysterically so that at least *someone* would know why he was there before he would be taken away to suffer a terrible execution.

"Escape from this place? From Wilhelmstaße?" she asked him, equally frenzied before Gestern and Haupt heard the commotion.

"No, no, from 1944! I cannot die here! I have to find Helmut Kämpfe and return to 2015!" Purdue pleaded in the lowest volume he could convey his panic to Maria. "Please help me. I'll tell you what is going to happen and you will look like a goddess to Hitler!"

"You are insane," she frowned, pushing the babbling Scotsman away. She called for the two officers to come and get him, so that she could assist Sigrun and prevent her from biting off her tongue.

"Come on," Haupt smiled, "to the cells until Diekmann is back to speak to you."

They tied Purdue's reddened wrists behind his back and walked him to the other side of the hallway, down a short spill of steps and into a dark passage lined with only four cells. Purdue coughed profusely from the pungent stench that came from the second cell they passed.

"Oh, you like that smell?" Gestern asked. "Sturmbannführer Haupt, I believe David Purdue wants cell B."

"I don't see why not, Sturmbannführer Gestern," Haupt replied in a put on voice. "He did show up here uninvited after all, ja? Cell B is our special cell for unwelcome guests."

"See? That was Captain Jan Markgraaf, a Dutch fighter pilot flying reconnaissance for the RAF," Gestern related like a proper tourist guide. "When the Luftwaffe shot down his plane over the border he flew with that damaged Spitfire as far as he could until he had to jump out! Captain Markgraaf landed right in the middle of Berlin with his parachute. Imagine that!"

"He just showed up without an invitation too, so I think you should be roommates, right?" Sturmbannführer Gestern suggested. Purdue was too tired, upset and sore to fight them off. He simply allowed them to cast him into the rotting cell where the remains of a man sat bundled and wet on the floor. Purdue ignored his burning skin to convulse on his knees.

"Oh, that's a pity. At least he won't smell that puke all night. By the way, David, dinner is at six!" he heard the officers laughing as they walked away. They closed the door behind them and left the injured Purdue in pitch darkness, overcome by fear and plagued by decay.

"Think, think," he whispered in the darkness. He tried his utmost best to compose himself. "It profits you nothing to panic, old boy. You agreed to do this for the glory of Tesla, of Lydia and mostly for yourself."

He was cold, but draping the army blanket of the bunk over his shoulders was extremely painful. All he could hear was a dripping tap against tin somewhere down the passage. "Hello!" he called, but only his echo answered; the echo and the drip-drip of the tap. He ached for water, especially to ease the waves of heat from the burns, but they were Nazi's. They left him to suffer and to hear that tap dripping, leaking precious liquid he could not reach to quench his thirst.

$\mathcal{N}$ ina sat in the dead silence of her guest room. Now and then she could see the flashing light of the lightning manifest through the tiny linear chasms in the iron sheeting where it did not quite come together when fixed to the windows. The whole house was soundproof and though fascinating, she found it decidedly morbid not to be able to hear the thunder or the rain, the howl of the wind, traffic or even just crickets on a quiet night. That was, assuming there were any bugs alive in the dead misery of the abandoned garden. Opting not to try and open a window on this stormy night, she surrendered to the fatigue of travelling she still had not shaken and retired to bed with earphones plugged into her iPod for some sanity from the massive tomb that enveloped her this night.

Everyone had turned in, apart from Sam who took the first watch at the chamber, should Purdue make contact. They had three days - probably less - to make contact with Purdue, ascertain his situation and location, direct him to Helmut Kämpfe to obtain the schematics for Tesla's *death ray* by any means necessary and to pulse him back to the chamber in Jenner Manor before the time is up. He checked his watch, finger at the ready on his recording device and he realized a chilling fact .

Day one had just passed.

They had two days left or else they would be arranging a nice secret ceremony, just Nina and him, to mourn their friend and occasional employer. Since Sam had completed his task for the Cornwall Institute he removed the battery from his phone soon after he was picked up by Purdue and Healy. It was better that way, not to be bothered until he had sorted out the conundrum with Lydia and Purdue's subsequent unintended trip that only escalated the problem. In the dense silence Sam sat wondering if Lydia's routine experiment really was an accident. She was far too much of a control freak to allow accidents, he figured.

That need slowly crept over him as he watched the minutes passed and his hand sank into his pants pocket, rummaging for his pack of smokes.

"Thank God she lets me smoke in here," he said to himself as he lit the first of only six left for the night, a most disconcerting feeling. He guessed that Lydia knew exactly what she was doing up until the power cut came. That kind of reaction was not one of a woman in control, but as soon as Purdue had gone up in flames she was calm as a drugged up college girl.

In his boredom he reckoned it would do no harm to reassemble his cell phone, if only to entertain him through what was probably the longest night of the world. He wished Nina could join him down here, but she needed to be fresh and rested in the morning to help Lydia pin Purdue's likely advancement according to historical incidents. Once he slipped in the phone battery he waited for the device to boot. The small light of the screen was a welcome sight here in the uniform lighting of the basement area that made him feel like a hostage in some desert bomb shelter.

No Service

"Of course. Fucking plated to keep the big bad world out," he scoffed.

The smoke snaked upward, unperturbed thanks to the lack of moving air. Against Lydia's rules for the night, he stepped out onto the back porch briefly to get a signal. With his back to the yard he could keep his eye on the small window he had forced open. If Purdue showed up in any form of light, the crack in the basement window would reveal it. His phone picked up a signal of three bars. "Good enough."

Sam's fag hung loosely between his lips as he pinched one eye shut to shield it from the smoke and he punched in his password.

One Voice Message

HE RETRIEVED THE VOICEMAIL, but he hoped that he would be able to hear it with the shattering sound of hail and thunder around him. The first part was a bit hard to hear —

'This is Albert Tägtgren, the idiot who foolishly trusted you yesterday.'

"What?" Sam winced.

'You are a coward, Cleave! You don't even have the balls to pick up the phone, you bastard! I know what you did!'

Sam could not believe what he heard. Why the hell was the Swedish nerd so pissed at him? *'And you knew I could not implicate you, because then my employers would know that I told you about the storage container and what I saw there. I am going to track you down and we will sort this out, you and I. You can count on that!'*

"Holy shit! What are you on about, mate? Jesus!" Sam

frowned, dodging the angry lightning before cowering into the kitchen and closing the back door as if he was never there. He closed the small basement window also, recovering the glass with the sheeting he had removed. But there was a bad taste in his mouth about the Tägtgren tirade. His first thought was to call the engineer back, but he was pressed for time to get back inside the manor and it would be rude to wake the man in the wee hours.

With a ripping propensity to sort out problematic things immediately after catching wind of them, Sam was trapped in a soundless, lonely purgatory. He kept mulling around the awful words he was almost sure he heard correctly given the static of the original call and the cacophony of his own environment while listening. But one thing was for sure; Tägtgren was out to get him and it would be wise of Sam to either stay underground until Purdue's two days had passed. Whether these days passed well or end in tragedy did not change the fact that the engineer had a grudge against him, for what, he did not know.

It prompted Sam to activate his paranoia a little bit more, but he was not about to tell the others about it. They had enough to focus their absolute attention on for the next forty eight hour fame. But adding to Sam's personal concern was the fact that Lydia did not trust him enough to allow him to leave, unless she sent her guard dog with him. By the looks of her procedures he and Nina had become no more than glorified, well fed hostages until Purdue could return. Only he could absolve them of the possible glory hounding they apparently would perpetrate through the eyes of Lydia Jenner if she let them out without a leash.

Clearly the professor was afraid that Sam would use the footage to claim his own credit on her design, her mastery. Now Nina knew of it too, which Sam felt amply guilty about. Lydia would also do everything to keep Nina close, lest she wrote a book on it or use the schematics Sam recorded to steal Lydia's fame.

On the other hand, Sam figured, the bitch would die soon and she was frail enough to perish for the slightest reasons. "Oh my God, Sam, you are John Christie and this is 10 Rillington Place!"

"It is?" Nina asked from a few feet away, giving Sam a tremendous start.

"Thank you, Nina. Healy would have to chuck these trousers now," Sam gasped.

Nina had a good giggle at the simile and bummed a smoke from Sam.

"I can't sleep," she sighed, blowing out the wonderful poisonous vapor. "This place creeps me out. It is as if the building cannot decide if it wasn't to be a home or a hospital. Did you see all those drips and medical boxes on the first floor?" Nina shuddered visibly.

"Aye, I must say I agree that this house feels like a giant experiment and we are the mice," Sam agreed, having another smoke. Nina's big dark eyes pierced his with a look of frustration Sam knew all too well.

"Thank you, Sam. That fright I gave you just then? I'd say we're even now."

"I'm just stating the obvious," he shrugged.

"But again, *you* brought me here. Don't start with shit like how we are mice in a maze bound to get hunted by some fucking cancerous Minotaur and her pet butler, after you promised my life was not going to be in danger," she whispered frantically in reprimand of him.

"I believe I said this is not a treasure hunt. We'd not be on expeditions with U-boats and caverns and huge *Ubermensch* bastards chasing us," he explained.

Suddenly they heard a tremendous clap. Both Nina and Sam jumped. By reflex Sam clicked on his video camera as they both sat spellbound, trying to see or hear the cause of the sound again.

"Was that...Purdue?" she whispered.

"Don't know. Listen. Do you hear that?" Sam asked. Nina nodded. They both heard a soft hum that fluctuated almost imperceptibly in tone every two or three seconds. Gradually, in the eternity it felt like to Sam and Nina, it grew louder into a deafening shudder of electrical current.

"Purdue?" Nina cried out.

"No use. I think we can only hear him, right?" Sam told her.

A crackle enveloped a faint sound that did not resemble the overlaying buzz. T came softly, grew exceedingly loud for about a second, and waned instantly afterward, yet the hum remained as if still in contact.

"—am, Lyd...Wilhelmstra— no Helmut..." and then came the last words that devastated Sam and Nina.

"So—hungry..."

The hum fizzled into a mere sporadic sputter and then the silence smothered them, feeling a hundred fold deader than before. Nina wept.

"Was that him? Was that a message? Did we successfully make contact?" they heard Lydia's thick voice approaching among the squeak of her wheelchair. "I heard that clap up in my room. By God, it takes forever to get down here without Healy!"

"Where is Healy?" Sam asked.

"Gone out for a few hours to meet a friend. I rather don't ask. He is probably gay," she shrugged nonchalantly. "Sam! Did you get that on video?"

"I did, aye."

"Please let me see. Let me hear him," she smiled. Nina was sobbing. Lydia put her stick-like arm protectively around the small slouching historian. "I don't mean to sound cold, Nina.

I am very worried about our friend. But he is resourceful and nothing short of brilliant. He will get back to us. I know it."

"Lydia," Nina snapped, "he had better come back or I am pushing your skinny ass into that precious fucking chamber of yours and sending you straight to hell!"

Sam winced at the expected chick fight he would have to break up, but to his surprise Lydia accepted Nina's threat and just removed her arm from the furious woman. Black smudges stained Nina's lower lids and her angry eyes were reddened with upset. Lydia did not want to push Sam for the footage, giving Nina a minute. She hoped the historian could appreciate that the professor did not hasten to see the testament to her genius for her sensitivity to Purdue's plight.

"I love him too, Nina. This is not half as selfish as you might think. But I am too fatigued to lock horns with you right now. Do not mistake my equable demeanor as acceptance of your hostility," she warned with gritty confidence, "even less as recoil."

Nina ignored the reprimand for now. She was too distraught.

"Now, Sam, please let me see the footage," Lydia asked politely, wheeling her way to the journalist's side. Nina grabbed another of Sam's cigarettes, but he did not mind this once, given how dismayed she was.

As he replayed the transmission to Lydia, Nina could not bear hearing Purdue's voice again. To her he sounded like an EVP from a ghost hunting show. Her former lover, her close friend and protector, Dave Purdue, was now reduced to a distant electronic voice phenomenon.

"Nina, do you not understand what we have achieved here?" she asked sincerely.

"I get it, Lydia. I fucking get it! But do you understand that Purdue might be trapped in a violent world alone, without any help, while you sing hymns to your precious fucking Tesla?" Nina shrieked, gesturing with her cigarette between her fingers.

Lydia had no retort. Dr. Gould was right. Lydia's efforts were all in honor of Nikola Tesla and his legacy, as well as her own. Nina could see this fact in the professor's formless eyes and with a flick of the cigarette she stormed off.

CHAPTER 20

*A*fter the terrifying night had passed for Purdue he had only a nightmare to look forward to. Within two hours after the SS officers had hurled him into the reeking cell with the decomposing corpse of the Allied pilot Purdue made an active effort to contact Lydia. In all his delirium and fear, the anguish of his scalded skin was far from dulled, yet he persisted in his slow moving crawl toward the largest space in the small cell. Where he could find an open piece of floor without debris or soiled linen strewn upon it, he placed the BAT.

Purdue had never been a religious man, but if he prayed for success in contacting his old friend there had to be some god looking out for him. In fact, as he mentally prepared the right words for his maiden broadcast with his finger tip on the button, he absolutely doubted the efficiency of the device. With no hope and only disappointment for causing his own misery in pursuit of grandeur, Purdue closed his eyes and whispered, "If You exist, whatever You are, I beg for your grace."

By no means did it mean he would believe in God if it

worked, but in some curious way he needed to ask some invisible force for courage. In the empty dungeon of cells and rot and mold under the godforsaken boots of the most evil men history had ever known, Purdue systematically did what he recalled Lydia telling him to do. It took him two hours to remember what the BAT box was for, and he also finally recovered the memory of what the dental plate was doing in his mouth. Relieved about the solving of the latter confusion, he pressed the covered button and virtually dropped the BAT in fear of holding the dangerous gadget in his grasp for too long.

The burns he had already suffered were intense enough. Purdue was not eager to find out what the sun's core heat felt like in the palm of one's hands! What baffled him was that the blinding light, reminiscent of the excessive thermal quality of the BAT left absolutely no residue on the floor or affected its surroundings whatsoever. He had merely spoken near the device, carefully choosing words that could consti-tute a briefing of significant information, but in truth Purdue had no idea if his message was ever received by Lydia – by anyone.

Of all things besides food, of course, Purdue wished for a hot bath. He was certainly too wary to ask the Nazi's for a shower, especially with their twisted forms of disregard for the lives of others. No sooner had he thought about the cruelty of the SS when the steel bolted door opened and let in the sharp beam of light. Purdue covered his face as the light stung his eyes, but the troops who came to collect him were worse off. Unaware of the state of the cells the two new soldiers were unfortunate to be confronted with a rush of sickening smells.

They coughed. One gagged and bent over to the side to throw up, but only delivered bile. Exclamations of disbelief and curses escaped them as they stumbled deeper into the dark passage to locate the Allied soldier they were sent to bring back to Sturmbannführer Adolf Diekmann. The men covered their mouths and noses with their sleeves to prevent the vile odor of decomposition from overwhelming them. To make things worse there was an underlying smell of electrical wiring gone faulty, but there was no electricity down here.

"Hello!" the one greeted the prisoner found seated on the floor with an army blanket wrapped around his body and his legs pulled in. He made no sound, but he was alive and awake.

"You are wanted in the administration office," the other informed Purdue.

'Administration office?' Purdue thought to himself. 'So no torture chamber?'

"Mein Gott! You smell terrible!" the officer cried, turning his head away from the bundled up blanket around their captive. Purdue wanted to lash out and blame the neglect of the SS for his condition, but he knew it would be futile. If anything it would only provoke their cruelty even more. The rumbling in his stomach only reminded him of the systematic abuse they inflicted on him.

"Can I get some water, please?" Purdue asked, hardly able to speak from the sandpaper in his throat. They ignored him, rambling on between the two of them about something amusing he could not translate. "Can I get some water?" he repeated as the nearing exit blinded him. Still they paid Purdue no mind, dragging his weak and aching body off to the administration offices. Attempting to ascend the stairs with them, his legs failed him and he sank to his knees.

Maria came out of nowhere. She rushed to Purdue's aid and shouted harsh reprimands at the two soldiers, sending one rushing for a glass of water.

"David, are you alright?" she asked, hooking her arms

under his to support him on the steps while the other guard looked on.

"I'm so hungry, Maria. Please, anything to eat. Anything," he panted weakly.

"I'll get them to give you something to eat after your interrogation…"

"Please! Don't let them torture me! I'm not a soldier," he pleaded again. Purdue's face was an inch from Maria's beautiful countenance and his blue eyes were desperate enough to soften her heart. After his confession the day before she thought him a lunatic, but after much contemplation throughout the evening Maria had to reconsider. After all, she herself was a medium, channeling spirits and touching other worlds all the time. She had no right to dismiss him as a deluded maniac.

When she went to speak to him in the late hours of the night she saw a blinding white light exude from under the door of the holding cells. It was unlike anything she had ever seen, almost something she would have construed as unearthly. On seeing this phenomenon, knowing that only David Purdue was inside, she withdrew. Even with her insatiable curiosity as to what happened inside, she did not think it wise to enquire and draw attention from the guards. They were too meager of reason to understand.

"I am afraid I cannot promise that, David. But know this…" she looked at the attending soldier waiting for the other to return with water. He was distracted by a verbal altercation in one of the offices. "…I know there is something supernatural about you."

"But…" he lit up, eager to elaborate, but she hushed him. She shook her head, frowning at her erroneous choice of words. "Not supernatural, but unusual."

"I told you yesterday, Maria," he started, but the other guard showed up with a tall glass of water. He crouched down and gave Purdue the water, but he clearly did not want to. It would have been great entertainment to watch the Allied intruder suffer, but they all knew that Maria was not to be crossed. Her potency was as great as her beauty. With Sigrun by her side, the two women headed the powerful Vril Society and had the ear of the Führer and Heinrich Himmler both.

"I need to know, David. I need to know everything," she whispered in his ear as he greedily guzzled down the soothing water. She stood up and addressed the two soldiers with authority. "Make sure that he does not spend another night without food or water."

With this she walked away and left Purdue to the mercy of the SS officers awaiting him in the large office at the end of the hall. Purdue had never experienced such terror in his life. Reading about the Second World War was like visiting the lion's den at the zoo – looking in at the carnage from the security of high walls and steel barriers. Now he had been denied the safety of the fence and he was the main meal.

It was an atrocious time of raw and brutal evil, a time wherein nobody was ever safe. Madness prevailed and insanity corrupted those in power to the obliteration of the masses. Not even Germans were safe if they were judged by the personal vendetta of any of the commanders. Here he was, about to be interrogated by one of Hitler's vicious beasts and his very fate was in the hands of a man who could end his life without lifting a finger.

The office was only that in name. Only three chairs surrounded a wooden desk with drawers in which the folders of prisoners, politics and enlisting documents were stored. But the rest of the room reeked of ammonia, floor polish and some awful whiff of formaldehyde mating with both to form nightmarish images in Purdue's mind.

'Don't be hostile. Don't speak out of turn, old boy,' he

instructed himself as he laid eyes on the Sturmbannführer seated at the desk. *'In fact, remember who you are.'*

"You are David Purdue?" the scrawny bald man with the laughing eyes asked.

"Yes, sir," Purdue answered over parched discolored lips. *'You are David fucking Purdue. You have more money than God and even more charisma. Command the room in the way only you know,'* his reason urged him.

He was numb with fear here in the presence of a Waffen SS Commander who had not a second thought for butchering women and children just to see their expressions. But he had to keep his wits about him. Purdue had to retain his positive nature, his cordial manner with which he could sway almost anyone to favor him.

Up until this very moment, through all his dangerous expeditions, his costly pursuits, reckless relic hunting and questionable associations, Purdue had never known doubt. Right up until this moment the affluent inventor and explorer had never tasted the choking venom of searing anguish. Never before had he abandoned his courage. There was always a way out, whether by the mercenary or by the wit. His money and his charm had always given him the upper hand, but now, in the snake pit of the SS, Purdue found himself a pauper.

CHAPTER 21

"*D*avid Purdue, I am Sturmbannführer Adolf Diekmann," the officer said calmly. "I believe you have managed to break into the Reichkanzlei without being caught. Actually," he said as he looked down at an open dossier before him, "it says here that you were not even seen coming in. What bothers me, Herr Purdue, is that you found your way through this Chancellery, past all the staff and officers and ended up in a bunker two floors below ground…" he locked his icy eyes with Purdue's, "…that was locked from the *outside.*"

Purdue felt his heart thunder in his chest. The two soldiers who escorted him here flanked the commander and leered at him. He had no idea how to respond. If he spoke the truth they would kill him just for insulting their intelligence and if he lied he would come across as a spy, or worse, an assassin out to murder Adolf Hitler.

"I am waiting for an explanation. You say you are not an Allied soldier like your cell mate, so what were you doing down there? And how did you come in?" Diekmann insisted a bit more firmly. Purdue knew he had to say something.

"I am an inventor, sir," Purdue employed his acting talent to appear convincingly humble and insignificant. "Do not let my nationality fool you. I am an avid follower of the late and brilliant Nikola Tesla, having assisted him on a few occasions with experiments of a secret and sensitive nature."

"Nikola Tesla. Nikola...Tesla," Diekmann sang, trying to place the familiar name.

"If I may, Sturmbannführer," one of the soldiers interrupted respectfully, "he was an American of great renown, specializing in the field of electricity and mechanical engineering. Died last year." The soldier lowered the volume of his voice and bent forward toward the level of Diekmann's ear, "Nikola Tesla was a close friend of George Viereck, Sturmbannführer."

That name, however, was very familiar to Adolf Diekmann.

"Ah! A friend of Viereck! And you worked with Tesla?" Diekmann asked, suddenly intrigued.

"Yes, sir," Purdue nodded, keeping to his mild and kind modesty. But in truth Purdue had no idea who the hell George Viereck was. He only hoped his decent knowledge of Nikola Tesla could give him a bit of an edge over Diekmann. For once he was thankful for the presence of the spiteful and antagonistic guards. Had the soldier not spoken up Diekmann would never have known who Tesla was, rendering Purdue's alibi worthless.

Diekmann was impressed. His gaunt cheeks fell into deep vertical wrinkles as he grinned with satisfaction. Indeed Viereck was a very prominent supporter of the Third Reich, having interviewed Hitler twice before and having delivered speeches in Berlin in honor of the Führer in his presence. Now he knew that Tesla was an ally, therefore any man who worked with him would be a friend of the Reich.

"So tell me, Herr Purdue, how did you get into the

Reichkanzlei?" the officer insisted.

Purdue had to think on his feet. He acted coy and smiled. Speaking under his breath as if he knew the secrets of the universe, he replied, "Please, sir, do not tell anyone yet that we had succeeded. You are the only man I am telling in confidence."

"Yes?" Diekmann pressed eagerly, too happy to be privy to this information.

"I conducted an experiment for being almost completely invisible," Purdue confessed.

"Invisible? But how?" Diekmann asked.

"If you do not mind, sir…it is an experiment I wish to perfect so that I can surprise the Führer with a new method to mobilize the troops unseen over borders and into the parliaments of the enemy," Purdue explained so realistically that he almost believed himself. Suddenly his old streaks emerged, his irresistible presentation that had always won him the support of even the most cynical of minds. "It could revolutionize the art of reconnaissance, intelligence….even assassination."

"Fantastisch!" Diekmann smiled.

Dave Purdue had found his guile and nerve again. Somehow he thought up the perfect excuse for his arrival in the Reichkanzlei at the drop of a hat. And since the SS, especially Hitler and Himmler, found the mysteries of science and the occult so fascinating it was easy for them to believe that such a thing was indeed possible with the right research and experimentation.

Diekmann fell for it all, but Purdue had to steer this matter in just the right direction or else he would never find Helmut to procure Tesla's notes before his time ran out. He needed to convince Diekmann that he, Purdue, knew the unknowable. If there was one thing Nina taught him about the secret societies it was that they were suckers for super humans and exceptional characters. And during his stint as Renatus of the Order of the Black Sun he learned a great deal from the Council of high members about the Nazi reverence for godhood or pursuit of it.

"If I may, sir..."

"Yes, Herr Purdue," Diekmann turned his head slightly as if to listen closely.

Purdue knew this ruse could end tragically for him, and wondered if he should not abandon the idea of stirring things up. But what he was going to have to impart on the commander would be the only way to prove to the SS command that he was in possession of special abilities. In truth he hoped he knew enough about German history to accurately 'predict' future events.

"I have another confession."

"And what is that?" Diekmann asked, looking a bit more suspicious this time.

"Um, I am a bit embarrassed to admit this, but I have this gift since birth...that I can..." he doubted the ridiculous claim he was about to make, being a fervent cynic of it.

"Yes, man! Speak," Diekmann shouted, having lost his patience at waiting.

"I can predict the future."

The two guards did everything in their power to keep a straight face while the commander stared at Purdue with a look of disappointment and a tinge of disdain.

"Take him away!" Diekmann shrieked. From both sides the guards seized Purdue and dragged him off. He could not believe that his apparent success had backfired so quickly. His escorts carelessly flung his sore body from one to the other, pushing him hard at the top of the stairs. Purdue staggered down the staircase, steered by the hard grips of the soldiers.

"You worked with Tesla? You can go invisible? Why don't

you do that right now, fool?" one shouted as they corralled him back towards the filthy cell he spent the night in.

"It doesn't work like that, you imbecile," Purdue scoffed with a smile. He insisted on keeping his defiance alive by condescending means. If he was going to die he would go out pestering them instead of cowering in a corner and weeping for mercy. For his insolence he received a jab to the face and a kick to the side of his knee which immobilized him completely. Purdue screamed in pain.

"We will be back to shoot you as soon as Sturmbann-führer Diekmann gives the order, British swine," he heard as he was thrown back into the darkness with his rotting room-mate. Purdue cried out in agony as his knees hit the cement and his elbow and palms slid under his weight.

'To hell with this shit!' he thought. *'I am attempting the travel back tonight! No more. Nothing is going to save me now that Dickwad smelled a rat!'*

Soon after they left him in the desolate black pit of stench to count the hours to his fateful end Purdue prepared to communicate. He intended to make contact only to warn Lydia and Sam that the next connection from him would be his return, provided that it actually worked again. Wincing in excruciating pain from his fresh injuries he kneeled on the floor where he previously placed the BAT. His body throbbed with intense pain, more now from his burned skin, but he did not care. This was one adventure Purdue did not want to continue. He could hardly see anything in the dense oblivion around him and it gave Purdue the sensation of weightlessness, of being lost at sea, in space. Whirling inside his skull his brain assumed that it was afloat in half death - that his body was falling a thousand miles per hour while suspended in a cold womb of madness.

Confusion born from sensory deprivation and untreated pain wrapped itself around Purdue's reason. Holding on desperately to his mission, his identity and of all things, his sanity, the once fun loving billionaire shed his hope. Only the timid light from under the steel door illuminated a part of the cell floor. The BAT was lying on the ground, but this time he doubted anything would come of his new ritual. In fact, Purdue had no idea if it even made contact with Lydia the first time.

With a weary, shivering sigh he pressed the button for the apparatus which started to glow.

"Here we go," he said, having not bothered to prepare specific words this time.

The cell lit up like the mid of day, ripping through his eyeballs before he closed his eyes, and he waited for the same hum he established before when he spoke his specific words into the atmosphere around him. Purdue wished that the bright light was his highway through time to get home, but diffused on the edges of the beam he could still see the cadaver with the dirty Dutch flag patched to his putrid coat. "I am in hell. Please God, don't let me stay behind here," he remarked at the hopeless sight.

'We won't leave you, Purdue.'

"What?" he gasped, sitting up and listening attentively. "WHAT?"

He heard the voice again, rising and falling through the static frequency like a ghost voice on a very old radio speaker. *'Come back.'*

Purdue's eyes welled up with tears and his body shook under the emotion. *'Nina?'*

Vaguely he heard Sam's words break up through the ether, but then a very loud and distinct sound punched through the void. It was Lydia. *'Dave, write this down! Go to Oradour-sur-Vayres! Helmut Kämpfe has the Tesla papers on him! The French Resistance will kidnap him tonight and hide him there!'*

'Come back! We'll wait for you!' Nina's voice fought over

Lydia's with seething fury.

A heated argument ensued over the radio waves before an abrupt cut in power that left Dave Purdue dressed in a cloak of dead quiet night again. His ears hissed from the intense sound that just left him and his eyes gradually adjusted to the darkness again. As the white noise instantly ceased he could have sworn he heard a loud crack, but with all the sounds around him he was uncertain. Purdue was elated to have heard Sam and Nina's voices reassuring him. Wiping his tears with his sleeve he quickly jotted down the details of Lydia's transmission, noticing that his writing in the darkness was legible. There was a source of light coming from the open steel door that started him. The door was open?

He leaned forward, slipping the BAT and the note back into his pockets. Two figures stood in the entrance. They stepped inside and came towards Purdue's cell. He was amazed to see Sigrun and Maria there, each holding a tray. Scrambling to get up, Purdue almost sprained his ankle. In all his life he had never starved like this.

"We brought you some food, David," Maria said. As usual, Sigrun said nothing. Her identical resemblance to Nina Gould was uncanny.

"Thank you," he grunted weakly, "so much."

They slipped the amply stocked trays through the narrow rectangle in the gate and he ripped through the meal like an animal.

"Not too fast," Sigrun said firmly. "You will die if your blood sugar rises too rapidly."

"David, we saw you basking in brilliant light," Maria told him in awe. Her eyes were filled with devotion and admiration, but Sigrun narrowed her eyes and smiled, "We know what you are now, what your essence is made of." She smiled kindly and caressed his face through the bars. "We welcome you to the Vril Society."

CHAPTER 22

"*A*re you seriously so selfish, Lydia?" Nina sneered right after the connection ceased. Sam held her by her arm to perturb her movement, keeping her from attacking Lydia.

"She is in a wheelchair, Nina!" he reminded her, but it had no effect on Nina's intent.

"I don't care if she is a fucking headless paraplegic, Sam," she hissed at him. "Her handicap does not give her the right to treat her friends like bait, like...like..." she caught her breath.

"Nina, he agreed of his own free will to do this for me," Lydia explained. Sam was surprised at how unusually composed she was, but it was hard to tell if her docility came from contrition or from control.

"I get that," Nina said, "but now he is in trouble and instead of allowing him to come back immediately you still have the audacity to send him on errands! From now on my task here is suspended. I am not advising you on any more details of the French massacres so that you can play remote recon with a friend of mine!"

"Listen, ladies, it is no use fighting over this. I propose we keep calm. We sit down like civilized professionals and we consider the factors before we decide what to do the next time he makes contact," Sam suggested.

"He could be dead by then," Nina retorted. "You heard him. He is in hell, he is hungry. God knows what else is happening to him that he just doesn't have time to tell us about."

Lydia sat quietly with her head bowed, contemplating the Tesla Experiment. It had come to the point where she had to decide what it was worth to her and if Purdue's life was truly of less importance than her glory. Even if she could not prove that Tesla's *Teleforce* weapon was a military marvel that could decimate the offensive forces of any invasion, she would still have proven that portals could safely transport humans between different spacetime fields.

"Perhaps that would be enough glory," she mumbled, spilling the sentence out loud to see how if it sounded acceptable to her ego.

"What would be enough glory?" Nina asked.

"To just have sent a man back in time, captured on film this time," she answered. "Maybe if we leave Tesla's schematics for the death ray to the past, uncompleted, it would pass into history as just a theory. Maybe leaving the design in the dust of World War II we might avoid World War III."

"Wait, what do you mean by 'sending a man back in time was captured on film *'this time'*?" Sam frowned. Nina stared at the frail, emaciated genius and wondered why the world's most brilliant minds always rested in the weakest vessels.

"That's the most sense you have made since I've met you," Nina told Lydia, folding her arms. "Leave the bloody weapon alone. Weapons never beget peace or power and you know it. But being known for making science fiction science fact is a far better feat. You know full well the maniacs in power these days are the last toddlers who should be given a loaded gun." Nina's voice had calmed considerably. She sat down next to Lydia's chair. "Bring him back, professor."

"What do you mean we filmed time travel *this time*, Lydia?" Sam repeated with more frustration. "Have you done this to someone else before? Is this why you had to send Purdue? You sent someone back before and let me guess – he failed to come back, didn't he?"

Lydia looked distraught. She simply dropped her eyes to the ground. Sam, aware that he was the one who promoted patience and self control a minute ago, grew annoyed at Lydia's non-response.

"Professor Jenner, I really must insist!" he said loudly, trying not to shout.

"Oh, Jesus Christ! Enough already!" Lydia growled. Her eyes almost disappeared under her scowling brow as she erupted. "What is it you want to hear, Sam Cleave? Does it sound like another juicy story for you to plant another petty prize on your mantle? Huh?" The professor bellowed like a beast in her deep rasp. She rolled her eyes and threw her head back, "Good God! I am so fed-up with people who do not appreciate the meaning of *sacrifice*! Sacrifice! A thing I know…" her voice broke and her breathing raced. Her quivering breath fell into words again. "It is a thing I know first-hand."

She turned her chair to face Sam squarely. "Don't you ever…*ever*…insinuate that I surrendered another to my obsession! My passion for science took my all, no-one else's. My quest to finish the unfinished left by a great, but cheated master has cost me everything," she cried, gesturing to her fragile body. "I gave everything because Tesla deserves the complete triumph he could not attain in his lifetime. So don't you dare insinuate, Sam, that I do not care what happens to

Dave where he is. David Purdue is the only man I know who understands sacrifice for one's passion like I do. And he knew the risks, but he went because he knows what it is like not to know – not to know if that *one* risk that seemed too much, could have been the door to the answers."

Sam had no comeback. She did not answer what he was really asking her, but she did make it crystal clear that she was not the self serving bitch they assumed she was. However, Nina, who had been listening closely to the spat, knew that answer.

"You don't have brain cancer, do you?" she asked the weeping woman. Nina's question sounded like an acknowledgement, more than any inquiry.

Lydia shook her head slowly from side to side, feeling an immense measure of relief to finally be able to tell someone.

"What do you mean?" Sam asked Nina.

"Jesus, Sam, you can be so slow sometimes," Nina sighed. She turned her attention to Lydia, who repeatedly breathed out deep sighs as she embraced her renewed release. The historian studied Lydia's condition with her eyes. With great concern and sympathy she asked, "Professor, is *this* going to happen to Purdue when he comes back through that…" she motioned to the chamber, "…doorway?"

Sam suddenly realized. "Wait, this is not a terminal illness, it is the effects of the Tesla Experiment?" He was astonished.

"Yes," Lydia admitted. "You can't exactly tell people you suffer from *Time Travel Syndrome* or whatever when you look like shit. I'm not even fifty yet and I look like a monster. So I cried cancer, and nobody batted an eyelid because it was a monster they knew. People don't like things they can't explain or prove, and they don't like people they cannot classify to put them at ease. If they think you have a terminal illness you have their permission to be broken."

"So the figure Albert Tägtgren saw going up in flames at CERN...that was *you?*" Sam asked. At the mention of the engineer's name his stomach sank, but he kept a straight face that hid his thoughts.

"That was me. But we did not film that one for the record, simply because it was so – unexpected," Lydia smiled bitterly. "I activated the particle fields with the capacitors in the container under Alice, because they were so much stronger than the type I had at my disposal. I never thought it would function; not in practice! It was not supposed to do anything but provide me with a tremendous electrical current so that I could test Tesla's accuracy on the prescribed amount of force."

"So what went wrong? Or right, perhaps?" Nina asked.

"Sound interfered," Lydia replied plainly. "Just the one element I did not calculate because it wasn't part of the experiment. The Tesla Experiment was mainly to measure the probability of the various components involved to produce the adequate voltage and acceleration to thrust the energy beam with enough force," she explained. "But the alarm went off in that section just as the force field achieved enough power. So, with the decibels of the alarm exceeding the threshold of the frequency it sounded on, the *teleforce* experiment resulted in an inadvertent discovery altogether."

"So instead of testing a prospective ray gun the unex-pected alarm caused time travel?" Nina asked in amazement. Lydia chuckled foolishly at the wonderfully simplified truth that sounded absolutely ludicrous.

"Strange, isn't it? And that is why I was adamant to obtain the original notes Nikola Tesla made on the so-called 'death ray' while I was...well, away. At least then I could build the machine he envisioned, not some apparatus devised by guesswork."

"Unbelievable!" I mean that," Nina exclaimed in wonder.

She hated admitting it to herself, but she saw Lydia Jenner in a completely different light now. No longer did she feel angry at Lydia's pursuit of the elusive notes. If her body was ravaged so utterly by an accident of physics, the least she could do was to use the discovered method to procure the original plan. It only bothered her that Purdue was the one scouting for it.

"And how did you come back, then?" Sam asked her, surreptitiously recording the story she told. "Surely you did not have the proper device, because you had not invented it yet."

"You're right," Lydia said. "I have to admit to my disgrace that I used seduction to get around while I was there. I met Helmut at a symposium relating to Armaments and when I mentioned Tesla's work on charged particle beam weapons, he bragged about having confiscated materials from Tesla's room after his death in 1943."

Sam was amused by her resourcefulness. "So you seduced him," he smiled.

"Seduced him? Honey, I rode him bareback," she winked, evoking their laughter at her forwardness. Her merry relation withered to a reminiscence of regret. "But I was there for far longer than I surmised, you see. That is partly why I ended up decaying physically like this. I lingered there for too long, so to speak. You see, within the ether there is no chronological order and so every destination visited by a traveler would hold a different rate of cellular regression, that which we call time."

"Aging?" Sam asked. "But you don't look old, just…"

"Sick," she nodded. "Think of it as a *desert storm*."

Sam looked as confused as Nina, but both were intrigued. Nina had forgotten about Purdue's predicament by now and Sam was worried about his memory card running out of space before Professor Jenner was done explaining.

"A desert storm? Do tell," Sam pressed.

"Well, imagine your body is a landscape of flat and loose sand, like a desert. Now imagine that one droplet of water falls for every day of your life," Lydia described slowly.

"I'm with you," Sam acknowledged.

Lydia continued, "Right. Now. What happened to me while in the ether - and the two days I spent with Helmut - is the equivalent of a rainstorm on my desert. Each particle of radiation, each cosmic ray, existent duration, thermal fluctuation, and so on and so forth, collided with and eroded the cellular aspects of my anatomy."

"Jesus," Nina whispered sympathetically.

"By the time I finally found my way back I arrived in the chamber, barely alive from cellular deterioration," Lydia shrugged. Carefully she rolled back her sleeves to reveal seared skin tissue. "The intense electrical current that facilitates entry into the ether 'highway' literally causes combustion, but fortunately it happens so rapidly that it rarely singes deeper than the epidermis."

"Oh, good!" Nina gasped. "Well, at least that's lucky."

Lydia gave Nina a weary leer and shook her head. "Your sarcasm is not welcome, Dr. Gould."

Sam chuckled at the banter between the ladies. Unlike their previous exchanges a milder, more amicable mood prevailed.

CHAPTER 23

"*W*ith respect, Frau Orsic, the man is insane. I can believe a scientifically possible stance, but really, to tell the future? It is madness! Not to mention that by such a claim he is ridiculing the acumen of the Waffen-SS and the High Command in general," Sturmbannführer Diekmann argued with Maria.

He was busy preparing for his company to move out toward Haute-Vienne and had only reported briefly in Berlin before rejoining the mobilization. As commander of the Waffen-SS, 1st Battalion, he would soon join his men in Southern France to help stop the Allied advance. Sturmbannführer Diekmann's battalion was part of the 4th SS Panzer Grenadier Regiment ("Der Führer") that served with the invasion of France.

"Please, Sturmbannführer, you have to listen to me. Sigrun and I both saw something unbelievable take place right in front of our eyes and Herr Purdue was its architect. Both the Führer and Reichsführer Himmler have agreed that you are to take Herr Purdue with you to the front," she retorted forcefully.

Adolf Diekmann was not about to be ordered around by a mere civilian woman with no significance in the Waffen-SS. He stepped forward, standing inches from Maria and sneered, "Let's get one thing straight. You might be a famous medium who runs one of our secret societies, talking to ghosts and channeling extra-terrestrial beings and I don't know what else, but if the Führer wishes me to dance to your puppetry, my dear, he would have to issue the order himself."

"Sturmbannführer," a subordinate officer greeted, holding a signed order from Heinrich Himmler. "This is for you, sir. Directly from the Reichsführer."

Maria smiled, only infuriating Diekmann even more with her satisfied glow. He grabbed the order stipulating Dave Purdue's accompaniment to the front with him, and perused it briefly. In the order it stated that Purdue had invaluable information to be advised.

Diekmann glared at the beautiful leader of the Vril Society and asked, "What does this imbecile possibly have that we need, Maria? If he could really tell the future he would have known that he was going to get captured inside the Reichkanzlei, wouldn't he?"

"Please listen, Adolf. Besides what I bore witness to, I know the Führer is behind him too. So, are you implying that the Führer is incompetent in his decisions?" she teased with a very serious undertone he dared not tempt.

"Of course not!" Diekmann bellowed. "What was it that convinced all of you to trust this man?"

She leaned towards him with her striking big eyes and glorious lips, "Herr Purdue told me that Sturmbannführer Helmut Kämpfe, commander of the 'Das Reich' division would be kidnapped by the French Resistance…tonight." Her whisper was positively chilling.

Diekmann chuckled in disbelief and shook his head at her. "That prediction does not signify that Purdue is psychic, my dear. It rather denotes that he is a spy. How else would he know the business of the Resistance?"

She could not rebut his statement. As his eyes danced from side to side on hers, she realized that he had a very fair point, yet she would not concede to it.

"There is more to him than this. I know what I saw," she reminded Diekmann. "Make sure he is well taken care of, would you? The Reichsführer is counting on your cooperation with regards to our newest member."

"He is part of the Vril Society now? He just waltzes in under suspicious circumstances, does one magic trick and now he is connected to the SS Elite?" Diekmann laughed skeptically. "Unglaublich!"

"If that chews at your ego, Adolf, then I suppose this next bit of news will have your head spinning," she smiled mockingly as he waited anxiously to hear what she had to say. "After telling the Führer what Purdue knew, and what we saw, and after he heard that Purdue worked with George Viereck's close friend Nikola Tesla, a meeting was arranged for next Sunday at Wewelsburg," she piled it on for him, each fact wounding his pride like a silver bullet. "Dave Purdue is being inducted into the prestigious Order of the Black Sun."

The revelation was so far beyond absurd that Diekmann simply sneered at her, pausing to take in the ridiculousness of it all. He looked at each of the stone faced soldiers in the room and finally headed toward the door, leaving Maria behind to gloat. As he exited the office he shouted casually, "Make sure he is ready tomorrow night at 21:00 Hours."

PURDUE SAT in his new cell, which had been cleaned along with the other three. The electrical lights illuminated the grey masonry and steel bunks in each cage and in the distance he could hear the occasional laughter of German conversation between officers and female staff of the Chancellery. Under his sleeves his skin had somewhat healed and the worst of the sting had subsided. No longer did Purdue have to catch his breath in agony every time he accidentally grazed against fabric or objects.

He sat in the otherwise quiet extension of the second floor below the city of Berlin, wondering what was going on above the ground. Purdue had been here many times in his life, but never before could he say he visited the square during the biggest modern war time in Germany. When he imagined that he could possibly run into the most evil Austrian of all time at any moment, Purdue was filled with both loathing and awe. To meet a historical figure of such significance would have to be the biggest moment of one's life, unless he was going to meet Adolf Hitler face to face just before taking his place in front of an SS firing squad. That would be a tragedy.

'What would Nina say if I had a picture taken with Himmler or Goebbels?' he pondered with a smile. It felt strange to smile again, especially amidst the constant fear for his fate. But Purdue hoped that Sigrun and Maria could liberate him at least from the cells, even if they planned to shove him back into the very cult he had been combating for most of his adult life, the *Black Sun.*

Since he was now more of a guest and less of a prisoner he was not as nervous about footfalls approaching his cell anymore. Ever since the two women left him earlier he had been wondering what was going to happen now that he let it leak to the High Command that he predicted the abduction of one of their officers. Of course he ran the risk of being marked a plain spy with intelligence on movements he could appear to be involved in, but if he played dumb for long enough the Vril Society was bound to protect him from the Waffen-SS.

All Purdue could do now was to withhold important information on upcoming incidents to use as a bargaining chip to keep him from harm. He would have to give them only what they needed to see that he had knowledge of the immediate future and not an ounce more, otherwise he would become redundant. On the other side of the steel door the commotion died down and the voices steadily grew silent. Purdue guessed that it was just past 11pm now.

"I think it is time for the evening prayer," Purdue muttered to himself, going down on his knees on the floor. One last time he glanced to the door to make sure nobody was coming. He placed the BAT on the floor in the corner and took a deep breath.

The steel door's bolt made a loud clang and footsteps sounded shortly after the heavy door creaked open. Light weight moving swiftly on small heels told Purdue that his visitor was female before he even saw her. To his surprise it was Sigrun, not Maria. In her dark, silent way she stood staring at him for a few seconds before even speaking.

"My God, you look just like her," he said softly.

"Who, Nina?" she asked confidently. It gave him chills how much she acted like Nina, that even her voice possessed that same intonation and challenge. He nodded and smiled, but she was not one to dwell on unimportant matters such as past lovers. Unlike Maria, Sigrun was more calculating, less emotional and all about getting to the point.

"I need you to do as you are told, Herr Purdue," she told him plainly. "Do not attempt to flee the men of the regiment you are going to accompany. It will derail the direction of what is to come."

"And what would that be?" he asked, intrigued by the mystery of her.

"The assassination of Hitler," she answered casually.

Purdue went into a whisper, his eyes darting toward the

door to check for unwanted company. "Sigrun, I hope you are not going to attempt this on your own?"

She smiled. That very same smile haunted his memories of Nina Gould when she still used to be his lover. It was a sensual show of power and self-confidence.

"Do you really think that women like us, women who cross dimensions and communicate across light years with only the force of our minds, would dirty our hands with the blood of a pig like Hitler?" she scoffed with that same smile, looking toward the door while her amusement dwindled again. "This afternoon late Helmut Kämpfe was kidnapped from his quarters and you are going with Sturmbannführer Diekmann to show them where he is held captive," she informed him evenly. "They now cast their lot with your supposed wisdom, having no idea that their future is just a history text book to you."

Purdue listened intently, amazed at what she knew and how nonchalantly she addressed what needed to be done. She bombarded him with more information he fought to memorize as she spoke.

"Listen, at the upcoming meeting with Himmler and Hitler to bring you into the Order, you must not protect yourself when the hit squad strikes. Your survival has indirectly thwarted our attempt on the Führer before – every single time, no matter how many times the incident had been repeated over different time frames."

"Jesus," Purdue frowned. "What the hell are you talking about?

"I am telling you to remain seated when they breach Wewelsburg, David Purdue," she purred like a mountain lion. "I'm telling you to die. It is for the good of the Reich and the people."

Purdue was dumbstruck, but like a news cast, Sigrun related what he needed to know. "First you are going to help the Panzer Division retrieve Sturmbannführer Kämpfe, but you do not…I repeat, *not*…take the schematics from him. He needs to live, to pass it on to us so that we can construct the death ray Nikola Tesla designed. Do you understand?"

Purdue's mouth was agape, his eyes wide and his brain unable to compute all Sigrun was imparting upon him. In astonishment he slowly recovered his reason.

"You want to use the death ray's destructive capabilities to destroy the Nazi hold and end the war?" he asked. It was rather noble of the Vril Society to take on Nazi Germany and with self sacrifice he could help destroy the Third Reich and all its mobile forces.

"No, you idiot!" she yelped just like Nina. "We want to topple Hitler and his High Commissioners, the SS and their propagators so that we can procure their armed forces. That is all we want to leave active. The Vril will use the armed forces of the Third Reich to utilize the super weapon designed by Tesla to conquer the nations."

Purdue did not know what to say. With Nina's beauty Sigrun bade him goodbye, "I shall see you at Wewelsburg, then. Wiedersehn."

"Like the Hydra," he said softly as he watched her walk away. Her long dark ponytail swayed like a pendulum behind her sensual frame. "Cut off the head of a dragon only to beget eight more. A tyrant falls just to pave the way for one far worse."

CHAPTER 24

*H*ealy cooked for a change. Ever since his employer had begun to invite people to her house by some miracle of mind, he had not had time to really prepare a good meal. There were so many things to take care of here since Dave Purdue, Sam Cleave and Nina Gould came to visit and help Professor Jenner with her obsessive experimentation. No longer did Healy only have house chores and errands to do. Now he had three rooms to clean and new flower arrangements to collect; he had to keep the kitchen stocked with more than just Lydia's special protein shakes and the odd take away hamper.

Shopping for groceries used to be a once a month thing and now it became a daily run for the eclectic needs of the guests. If he did not know better he would have thought that the always reclusive and anti-social Professor Jenner was actually enjoying having house guests. He had been in her employment for almost five years and not once had he ever heard her laughing and talking about trivialities with anyone as she did with Dr. Nina Gould. Usually she only had some-thing to say when she was faulting someone less intelligent for an assumption or when she had to explain a scientific principal. He could not believe that she knew anything about fly fishing, cognac or the Dallas Cowboys.

Every hour was a colorful change of discussion with Sam about headlining news in other countries, electronic equipment and UEFA league football. They had been here for no more than two days and already Healy felt the house light up with life, as if they were not guests, but boarders. In turn Sam and Nina spent time together during Lydia's compulsory day naps. Healy wondered if they were an item, but butlers had no place in asking.

He constantly stared at the fiery beauty Sam liked to argue with, listened to her astute manner when she vibrantly recounted old stories from history documents that would never be found in books to share with the world. Healy was always one for women a bit older than he, because he was raised by only his mother. Learning the value of respect, efficiency and discipline came from a feminine approach when he grew up. Perhaps this was why he managed perfectly to maintain his nurturing, emotional understanding while being perfectly capable of taking on the most ruthless bastards on God's earth with his bare hands.

Lydia chose his service and company because of just that – his ability to be both a strong character to lean on and a listener with gentle sensibilities.

"Hard at work, Jeeves?" Sam jested as he walked past the kitchen to the toilet, slapping the doorway as he went. Healy smiled. It was refreshing to have someone like Sam to talk to. The journalist was always up for a wager, a beer and a challenge while having no problem busting Healy's balls with playful insults that he thoroughly enjoyed.

The thunder clapped just outside the back door. Stirring the gravy on the stove, Healy's smile instantly disappeared. It was replaced by a wince of fear as he subconsciously hastened his stirring. Sam reappeared in the door a minute or so later.

"You alright?" he asked Healy. The butler responded only by looking toward the window where the blue and white flashes lit up the curtain with pulses of light.

"Ah!" Sam realized. "I don't like it much either, actually. Was almost struck three times in my life. Being Scottish is hazardous. Golf courses, fly fishing, Highland sword dancing...none of which is a good idea under Scottish weather conditions."

Healy chuckled, grateful for the distraction.

"So, how is the beer in this town? I was thinking of getting us a six pack or two while we sit on guard at the chamber," Sam asked.

"Not bad, sir. I have a friend who owns a liquor store that stocks from Pilsen and Prague which is excellent. Not that pissy stuff, if you get my meaning," Healy said, sounding out of place talking about heavy beer in his refined British accent.

"Sounds good. Pull the pot on the other plate, my friend. You are going to escort me to said shop. If I have to spend one more hour drinking wine I'm going to kill myself," Sam announced zestfully. "Come, my good man!"

Healy reported to Lydia, asking her permission to accompany Mr. Cleave to stock up on beer before the next severe weather was due.

"Oh absolutely. He has been driving us insane with his whining over beer, draughts, real beer, weak beer..." she told her butler while Nina nodded in agreement as she dove into another glass of whatever French wine Lydia had her sampling this time round.

"Don't take too long, you two," Lydia called after Healy as he joined Sam at the door. "Purdue should report anytime in the next three hours."

"Trust me, I don't want to take three hours to get back before I can hear that hiss of a newly opened beer," Sam replied. "We'll be back shortly."

After the men left, Nina finally had to satisfy her curiosity. "Lydia, what's the deal with Healy and thunderstorms?"

"Ha! I see you noticed that," Lydia remarked. "From what I know about my darling butler - and I do not know half as much as I should about his clandestine past - is that he saw his mother struck by a bolt thicker than a tree trunk when he was a teenager."

"Oh my God! That is so sad," Nina frowned with sympathy for the attractive man who always looked a bit lost or lonely under his painfully neat, stern exterior.

"But I got that from his sister. She was here for a weekend with her husband once and we got talking while the men were catching a football match. That's when she told me. But, you know, we all have our secrets and our fears. I don't pry for more than what affects me directly and so I left it at that," Lydia shrugged.

～

THE RAIN WAS AMPLE, but light enough to navigate through the streets without too much trouble. Healy seemed nervous, Sam noticed, but with constant questions about places of interest he kept Healy's mind occupied so that he would not hear the odd rumble of the skies.

"Where did you work before the Professor burdened you with her insanity?" Sam asked, smiling. Healy laughed, but his anxiousness was obvious.

"I was a security consultant for years after I left the military. My father was a colonel. His father was an admiral, so they expected me to enroll just after school so that I could complete my studies through the force. But I enjoy this job much more, even with the madam's moods and that pedantic nature of hers. Under it all she is really a sweet woman."

Sam was impressed by how fond the butler was of the professor. Most of the nicest subordinates, as he learned through journalism, usually turned hostile given a moment of mock privacy to vent about their employers, but not Healy. There was an innate loyalty about the rigid butler who had now turned into a proper caitiff. Healy was downright edgy, clutching at the steering wheel as they turned from the riverside lanes into the parking lot of a very dilapidated looking shopping complex in a decent neighborhood.

"No wonder they sell booze other places don't stock," Sam remarked. "I don't imagine the fuzz likes to bother here."

"You are exactly correct, sir," Healy agreed, looking around vigilantly. A clap of thunder had him shrugging, just about sinking into his seat. His eyes fluttered, but he recovered quickly. "Goddamn weather," he mumbled as they parked in the back.

"I'm sorry sir, but I don't park on that side. Twice now they smashed the wind shield and the second time they almost stole the vehicle," he apologized.

"No worries, Healy. Let's go get a yeast infection," Sam smiled, tapping the lackluster butler on the shoulder as he got out.

Dodging the shower, Sam never saw the enormous body of the man who struck him down with a crowbar. The journalist hit the gravely tar with a splitting headache so severe that he could not manage to open his eyes. While he tried with all his strength to sit up and find his bearings, his brain switched off. Healy raced around the car to catch Sam before his skull hit the dark grey tarmac, but the man who towered over him simply looked out for any witnesses.

"Help me, Foster!" Healy told the giant with the crowbar.

"I can't believe you still wear that Christian memorabilia while you do what you do."

"Even God needs killers, Healy. And even sinners deserve mercy," Foster delivered his sermon to the annoyed butler.

"Where are you taking him?" Healy asked as Foster, who tossed aside the crowbar and picked up Sam's limp body to hang him over his shoulder like a bag of potatoes.

"That is not your concern, is it?" he told his old friend.

"It is very much!" Healy insisted. "My job is on the line for this."

"Well, that was the same concern Albert Tägtgren had before Sam killed him, Healy. That poor man lost more than his job that day," Foster empathized. "Go home and tell his girlfriend anything you need to. Your money has been transferred, old boy. Adieu!"

Healy stood in the rain, drenched. As the large SUV pulled away with Sam Cleave inside, he regretted agreeing to the subterfuge, but he direly needed that kind of money. He earned well enough under Lydia's employ, but he was not about to give up a few thousand Euros for a stranger's well-being. Still, he wondered exactly how far Foster was planning to take matters with the alleged murderer. It was a bit too hard to believe though, that Sam was a killer. Yes, he was a hardened investigative journalist in constant scraps with very dangerous organizations and deadly arms dealers, but he was not the kind who would kill.

Healy stood still while in conflict about Sam's just deserts, not even flinching under the shattering thunder that threw bolts of lightning in his direction.

"Maybe I deserve to be struck, Mum," he said under his breath. The ex-SAS man still struggled to see Sam Cleave as a murderer, but he also knew Christian Foster to be a man with an impeccable moral compass, one not to judge easily, nor harshly. If Christian was pursuing Sam for killing someone there was hardly any reason to doubt him. Never had Healy ever been this torn with a decision he thought he made perhaps too hastily.

The thunder shook the windows of the liquor store where Sam was anxious to pick up his beer. It was open. Healy went inside to purchase it anyway, although he thought it was in poor taste to do so. While the weather grew worse Healy sat in the car, opening the container of brew. It felt nauseating and therapeutic at the same time to swallow away that first bitter mouthful to ease his guilt. One after the other Healy drank beer after beer in a miserable attempt at taming the cancerous remorse that infected his heart.

"I'm so sorry, Sam. I had to. I had to," he slurred after the fourth he tried to drown himself in. There had to be something he could do to purge him of this unfortunate position, because he had no idea how to explain his treachery to Lydia or Nina once he returned home.

CHAPTER 25

1 0 June 1944 – 08.54am

AS THE 2ND Panzer Division – Das Reich moved along through the countryside of Southern France, Purdue found himself in the leading Tiger S33 in the company of Sturm-bannführer Diekmann and his men.

The metal monsters tanked along the low hills, over the tall grass, decimating the smaller trees and brushed in their way. Under the sunny morning sky the convoy of the Waffen-SS roared slowly through the Haute-Vienne region. The night before was catastrophic for one of the commanders of the regiment, the very cause for the urgent advance toward Oradour-sur-Glane this day. Led by the blood thirsty commander of the 'Der Führer' unit the war machines slithered to the sleepy little village where Purdue told them their commander was being held captive.

"I am not going to lie to you, Herr Purdue," Diekmann told his new advisor, "I am not at all thrilled to bring you

THE TESLA EXPERIMENT

with me to the front. I do not trust you and I aim to kill you the moment you even smell of deceit."

Purdue expected this hostility, but he hoped that Diekmann would have changed his mind by now. "I understand, Sturmbannführer. I really do. But I assure you that I am not here to mar your duties and I will stay out of your way until you have accomplished your goal."

"Good. I have no time to play nursemaid to some Allied traitor who cannot decide which side he is on. There is little as evident of cowardice as a man who defends nothing for fear of severing unfruitful alliances," Sturmbannführer Diekmann clarified. "Now, I need to know where the French Resistance is keeping Sturmbannführer Kämpfe. You had better pray that we find him alive in the hands of your faction, or you will suffer a fate worse than death."

"I assure you, on my honor, that I am not affiliated with the French Resistance," Purdue maintained. "I have this information because I have a special gift for foreseeing the immediate future."

"That is well to say, but you are wasting that rubbish on a man who believes in science and logic and reason. There is no such thing as psychic ability and energy manipulation by means of thought!" he exclaimed.

"Yet your Führer has unquestionable faith in such a possibility," Purdue retorted mildly.

"Look, for what I think is that the Führer has been advised on many subjects by many people. Unfortunately the demonesses of the Vril Society have made full use of this sorcery to influence the already fertile admiration that our esteemed leader has for the occult and things like psychic power. That does not mean that we all blindly fall for those claims...and that includes yours."

"But how do you explain that I knew this about your colleague, Sturmbannführer Kämpfe?" Purdue asked, while

165

the crew in the hull listened without saying a word between them.

"That is very simple. You are a spy," Diekmann answered casually. "But since I do not trust you I have put in place some security measures, just in case you are indeed leading us into a compromising position."

"You have me in your grasp, Sturmbannführer Diekmann. Why on earth would I send you into an ambush? Not only would I be killed in the process with you, but you would obviously cut my throat the moment you catch wind of my betrayal. I would have to be an imbecile to lure you into battle," Purdue marveled. "It makes no sense why I would even have told you of the kidnapping or where your man is being held if I did not have good intentions toward the Waffen-SS and the Nazi Party. My work with Nazi sympathizers should prove that to you."

From one of the units behind them someone shouted.

"Hold on," Diekmann told Purdue. "Let me see what that is about."

From the hatch the thin commander emerged. He called halt to the others and climbed out of the tank to investigate. Purdue felt terribly uncomfortable among the men left in the hull with him. They were obviously talking about him, but he could only tell what they must be saying about him by the derisive way they looked at him.

'Talk about cabin fever,' he thought. *'I hope this goddamn day gives me a chance to be alone long enough to call Lydia. I have to find Helmut and get away. I have had more than enough culture here.'*

Purdue was especially nervous about his looming deadline. It was the third day of his inadvertent excursion and according to Lydia Jenner's calculations, the final day before his energy locked in permanently with the point in the *ether* where he was sent. He would not be able to return after a certain amount of cellular latching had been done to the tapestry in which he was caught. It was what most referred to as time, but Purdue understood by now, that time was merely a relative term. He had no way of telling how long three days in his world were in relation to what it was in this world. For all he knew he could already have forfeited his way back by measuring in the wrong units.

"One of the tanks has met with a technical problem," Diekmann told Purdue when he peeked from the hatch and asked the commander if there was something he could do to help. "But not the kind your engineering or esoteric could remedy," he added.

The tall, gaunt Diekmann stood with his hands lodged in his sides, waiting to hear if the last tank in line has any spare parts for the one that suffered a break in its track. It was not a terrible blow to their time, but enough to call a break while the mechanics tended to the problem.

"How far are we from the village, Sturmbannführer?" he asked Diekmann.

"About an hour away. Why?" he asked.

"Just curious. Knowing how peasants deal with a prisoner, I hope they do not remove him to another location during the night," Purdue said, trying to press the commander into hastening the repair. His time was running out and he needed every moment to recover the schematics and make it back to Lyon in 2015.

Diekmann laughed. It was a cold, vindictive chuckle that was in no way comforting to Purdue. "My dear Herr Purdue, you do not have much faith in your own abilities, do you?"

"How do you mean?" Purdue asked.

"With a clairvoyant in our midst it would surely not be a problem to find out where Kämpfe is being held if we should find out he was transferred, would we?" he mocked. Purdue smiled and nodded. He had to admit it was not exactly the best thought through suggestion on his part, at least not one that served his ruse of being psychic.

"All done, Sturmbannführer!" a soldier reported.

"Good!" Diekmann smiled. With the back of his hand he slapped Purdue playfully in the stomach. "Come on, man. We have a brother to liberate and a town to destroy!"

10 June 1944 – 6.48pm

Purdue felt sick to his stomach. In the smoke and pandemonium he tried to hide the overwhelming shock and sorrow he felt for the inhabitants of Oradour-sur-Glane. Absolute chaos had ensued since the Panzer Unit cordoned off all entry and exit points to the town and insisted on the villagers reporting to the commanders to have their papers checked. It was a common smokescreen the Nazi's used to pick a fight with the people they intended to slaughter. Somehow they figured that it justified a lawful execution of civilians under the pretense of smoking out illegals.

Purdue was of the opinion that the Nazi's were sincere in their insistence on documents while their men spread out through the peaceful little town to search for Sturmbannführer Kämpfe. They could not find him, to Purdue's dread. But it only antagonized the Panzer Division more to be unsuccessful in their task. At first he thought that Diekmann would immediately call for his execution, that he would be deemed a liar, but the commander used the excuse of Kämpfe's absence as a reason to unleash his hellish brutality on the town.

Subsequently, he ordered the town to be ravaged and the people killed. Purdue could do nothing to avert what he had caused. It devastated him that his information brought Diekmann's terrible wrath to this town, this town that he, Purdue, brought to their attention. As the violence showed its hideous face the billionaire scuttled for the safety of the empty tank that stood a distance from the Oradour church. All the soldiers from the S33 were on foot, mowing down men and women with machine gun fire.

Inside the steel belly of the war machine the normally cheerful and resourceful Dave Purdue sat weeping like a child while he listened to the children crying in the arms of fleeing mothers who would see no mercy from the evil of the German troops. The men had been shot dead in the middle of town, executed for hiding a captive of the French Resistance, even after they repeatedly assured Diekmann that they had nobody in their keep, especially not a German officer.

After growing tired of hearing the incessant pleas for mercy from the people who insisted that they had no affiliation with Kämpfe's kidnappers, Diekmann and his other commanders ordered that the women and children who were left to be shut into the church. Purdue clenched his fists over his eyes as the horrid screams and desperate begging from the women echoed in his ears. He could hear babies crying and young children calling for their mothers, some voices silenced in the thundering claps of gunshots.

"You did this!" Purdue wept in the solitude of the deserted armored vehicle. "You brought them here!" But his guilt would become even more horrific as the time passed with the rumbling crackle of the fire that engulfed the church and drowned out the screams inside. He pulled out the note on which he scribbled down Lydia's information. When he read the details his heart stopped. "Oh my God! Oh my God! No!"

On the paper he had scribbled the name of the town as Oradour-sur-Vayres, but misinformed Diekmann by telling them that the German officer, Helmut Kämpfe, was held at Oradour-sur-*Glane*.

"Oh Jesus, no. I made a mistake! I made a mistake that cost hundreds of civilians their lives!" Purdue wailed in the deafening clamor of the town's destruction. Buildings of stone that were once proud homes, stores and meeting places were now razed and crumbling under the fury of the Waffen-SS and its demonic commanders. Purdue could hear a German man outside, nearer than the others, laughing.

Purdue was done with cowering, and in the knowledge that this atrocity was befalling innocent people because of his wrongful information, he decided to do something about it. As terrified as he was, he exited the tank and crouched under a clump of trees nearby, watching the laughing soldier saunter over to a barn. Next to the yet untouched barn was a horse cart the German was heading for. Purdue's blood ran cold when he saw what the knife wielding soldier was stalking.

Under the horse cart sat a young girl in a blood stained dress, holding onto a goat for dear life. She had no idea that the German soldier had seen her, and Purdue saw how her bloodshot eyes stared at the burning bodies on the pile a slight distance from her. There was no way he was going to sit idly by and watch anymore. It was time for him to escape, and he hoped that the girl could read English.

The night was here and the flames only illuminated the terror of the town even more. Fallen buildings smoldered while the Germans laughed and bragged about their ransacking. Purdue caught his breath when he saw that the girl was watching him. He did not want her to associate him with the evil men he came with. He gestured for her to be quiet before he slipped up behind the soldier, the very man who was chuckling about him to his colleagues earlier that day. As the man reached the horse cart Purdue leapt. As he fell on the soldier he grabbed the hunting knife, hoping that the element of surprise would be to his advantage.

Purdue had never been one for violence, something he always left up to his bodyguards, but this called for a fight. The knife slipped from the soldier's hand into his and, without sparing a moment, Purdue drew the blade deep through the skin across his opponent's throat. He dropped his little note for the girl to find. As the soldier fell, Purdue dropped the little note for the girl to find.

With one last glance to the appalling result of his misinformation, Purdue fled with a heavy heart, hoping that the god he did not believe in would forgive him...because he himself never would.

CHAPTER 26

Sam woke up in a daze. His eyes felt thick and his head throbbed, but the worst of it was the agony of a pulled muscle between his neck and shoulder where a hefty blow had rendered him unconscious before. His face distorted in pain, but he made sure that he did not make a sound. So many times before he had been in a situation like this that it had almost become normal. As his memory returned gradually he remembered the promise of a good beer and the nervous butler who, it turned out, was not anxious about the lightning after all.

"Bastard," Sam whispered, recalling Healy's betrayal.

In the dark of his surroundings Sam took his time to test the restraints he probably had wrapped around his ankles and wrists. But to his surprise he found that he was not bound at all. He could see nothing, but he could smell new carpets and a whiff of perfume. With a groan of effort Sam sat and tightened his abs to sit up, but his head instantly pounded with a sharp sting he could not endure and he quickly returned to his old position. The mattress he was lying on was soft, but the perfumed air had him worried about what was lying next to him.

He wondered how long he had been here, wherever here was, and then he thought of the ladies waiting for him in Lyon. It would be terrible if Healy had the same hostility planned for them that he had for Sam, for some reason. Sam shook his head to get rid of the ringing in his ears. Voices came from far off. One was male, the other female. He recognized the female voice.

"Penny?" he frowned. "What the hell...?"

They drew nearer. Sam rolled gently off the bed as not to be pummeled by the deadly headache again. On his knees on the thick carpet he inched himself closer to the sound of the muffled voices. By a few more paces on his knees, keeping his body low to the ground, Sam reached a corner that hugged his frame comfortably. From there he could hear them better.

"Please tell me you did not kill him in front of everyone," Penny said.

"Bitch," Sam whispered in disbelief of the woman he thought was just a professional who needed his services.

"Sam Cleave is a celebrity, you know," she told the man. "We can never be associated with his death, Christian! Nobody should even find him, actually."

"Who the hell is Christian?" Sam whispered.

"My dear, you are too hasty in your judgment," Christian Foster reminded her. "I did not kill him. I do not wish to kill him until we know for sure that he is the man you are looking for."

"I like this Christian bloke," Sam nodded to himself, trying to remember if he had ever encountered someone by that name before, someone he could have vexed into doing this to him. He had no idea why he had been kidnapped or why Penny Richards wanted him dead. He had not done anything to justify her wrath, as far as he could tell.

"Listen to me," she said, "he is the man we are looking for. He was the last person to see Albert Tägtgren alive. Who else would have killed him?"

Sam gasped. "Tägtgren is dead?"

"I don't know," Foster said. "I just think we should interrogate the journalist before we just make away with him. See what he has, what he knows. If we are satisfied that he is guilty, even by association, I will make him disappear forever."

'The phone call,' Sam thought. *'He wanted to kick my ass for something.'*

"Alright, see if you can find out where he is staying at the moment so that we can confiscate his gear. Once we have checked all the footage we will know for sure if he edited out anything important before sending it to me. He cannot know about the Tesla Experiment or our competition will have us by the short and curly's, do you understand?" Penny instructed.

Sam tried to make sense of it. Now he understood why the Cornwall Institute hired him. But he still could not figure out who made Tägtgren believe that Sam had spilled his secret to anyone. Someone had to have seen them together; someone who knew what they did. That was the person who probably killed Tägtgren for telling Sam. *'Penny knew, from what she just said,'* he reckoned. *'Healy also knows about the Tesla Experiment and I know how underhanded he is now.'*

Perplexed, Sam sat in the dark room with his hands on his wet hair. The warmth of his palms soothed his headache as he listened to the two in the next room. When he had enough strength he stood up against the wall to feel for a light switch, but found nothing but smooth paint under his probing fingers. In the back of his mind Sam knew that he had to escape as soon as he was able. Whatever his enormous captor had in mind, he had Jenner Manor in his sights next and Healy was definitely not going to protect Lydia and Nina anymore.

"Find out from Healy if he can obtain Sam Cleave's equipment without being discovered," Penny told Foster. "You can use the phone in my office. It has a scrambler so that we cannot be found by any tracers."

"Alright. I'll be back shortly," he agreed, leaving her alone in the adjacent room. Now was the opportune time for Sam to act. Penny by herself would be no problem to subdue, but once the big brute returned it would be virtually impossible to make an escape before Healy got to Lydia and Nina.

Sam used his entire bodyweight to thump against the wall where he was crouched before. He knew the sound would provoke Penny to investigate. Every time Sam hurled himself against the wall, he moaned from the sharp shooting pain in his head and the strain on his traps. But a little pain was nothing to bear in comparison of what would happen to him if he waited to be questioned – and likely get killed.

Now he truly realized why Lydia was so adamant on using Purdue to help her with the Tesla Experiment. It was obvious that she could not trust anyone else who knew about it. Penny was quiet, listening for the irregular bangs in the room where she told Foster to leave Sam Cleave. She could hear him whimpering in agony, and she did not want him to attempt anything stupid to keep her from finding out what he knew. Her own husband committed suicide for fear of having his secrets discovered years ago, so such measures were the first to surface in her reasoning with the sounds of pain she could hear in the next room.

"No, you don't," she said.

Penny's staff did not realize her involvement in the protection of the Tesla Experiment. It was a secret only known to the few people who funded it, attempted it and designed the means to put it into practice. Penny was part of the funding side over the years leading up to its fruition.

When she came to the door of the store room she roughly converted to Sam's holding cell she took a last look around to make sure nobody at the Cornwall Institute's local branch saw her. That was fortunate for Sam too, because there were no witnesses to see him jerk her inside the moment she opened the door.

"What is this about, Penny? I did not kill anybody. I did not even know that Tägtgren was dead! He sent me a threatening message, that I leaked his involvement and I cost him his job." Sam revealed, holding his hand over her mouth. He had Penny in a bear hug from behind to restrain her movement and he kicked the door shut. Penny said something into his hand.

"If you scream I will hurt you, I swear," he said, and she nodded.

Slowly he lifted his hand. "Who else knows about you filming there?"

"Just Healy and a friend of mine, David Purdue, but he is…" Sam cut the rest short, since explaining Purdue's whereabouts would take way too long.

"Then Healy could be the killer. He had no problem handing you over," she speculated. "What did you do with the real footage, Sam?"

"I don't have time to explain now," Sam said. "Give me your car keys."

"No."

"Penny, give me your car keys," he repeated, pulling her hair to manipulate her movement.

"I will not! You have no choice but to…"

Sam punched her lights out. Penny's body fell limply against him.

"I'm sorry, old girl," he whispered. "I just don't have time to listen to you shite right now."

He left Penny in the room and latched the door on the outside. Christian Foster would be on his way back by now, so Sam slipped through the rest room to another door that led past Penny's office. There Foster stood, talking on the phone. Sam's phone was probably still in Foster's possession. Keeping an eye on the huge man in the office, Sam entered the open laboratory and scanned the place for a suitable weapon. An iron bar holding up a makeshift shelf against the wall looked ideal. Gently lowering the shelf, Sam removed the bar and stole back to the hallway.

He stood next to the doorway, waiting for Foster to come through it. Sam's hands tightened around the bar as he sank to his haunches to be just about the height of Foster's knees. Holding his breath, he listened for the footsteps of his target drawing nearer as his heart pounded wildly in anticipation. With all his might Sam swung the bar against the assassin's legs, sending Foster howling in pain, writhing on the floor. With another blow to his head, Sam incapacitated him. He searched Foster and retrieved his cell phone.

With time to call for help Sam quietly passed through the hallways of the building, past employees and filing clerks. He tried to look as natural as possible, considering he sported a few bruises and nursed a headache from hell. Finally he made it to the lobby, dialing the only person he knew in this part of the planet.

Within ten minutes Sam was rescued by Professor West-dijk. It was a matter of luck that Sam recalled the old man telling him he would be taking a few days off in Bourgoin-Jallieu until the end of the month. His only friend at CERN collected Sam to take him back to Jenner Manor. Two blocks into his escape Sam noticed that they were being followed by a red Mercedes that quickly caught up with them. It was difficult to outrun the red car in traffic, and Sam could see that it was Foster sitting behind them. As soon as they were on the highway the chase continued at high speed.

Sam was impressed with Prof. Westdijk's driving. He kept Foster at bay for a good 10km further. A call came through on his cell phone.

"Are you alright, Sam?" Nina asked. "Where are you?"

"Nina, don't trust Healy! Don't open the gates for anyone! I'll explain later," Sam told her urgently. "We'll be there shortly."

"We?" Nina asked. But Sam had hung up already.

"Where are they?" Lydia asked.

"Sam sounds frantic," Nina said. Her voice was fraught with worry. "I know that tone of his, Lydia. It is not something to take lightly. He says we mustn't trust Healy."

"Bullshit. Healy would never do anything to hurt me," Lydia disagreed.

"Think about it!" Nina forced. "Healy stays away for the first time in how many years to catch up with a friend…just about the time that you send Purdue back? Just before you plan to finally get the Tesla schematics?"

Lydia had to concede. The time frames would coincide. Healy did change slightly when Purdue agreed to help with the experiment, although she did not think he was at all concerned about her work. In fact, Lydia reckoned Healy was a little jealous of the attention she got from Purdue and that was the reason for his slightly cooler behavior. Then again, Healy was not a warm, fuzzy man to begin with and it was difficult to tell how he felt most of the time anyway.

"Nobody knows that you are still alive, right? Those who knew you were working on the theories, Lydia, did they know you came back at all?" Nina asked.

"No. They had no idea that I survived the CERN accident," Lydia said after some thought.

"There you go. Healy waited until you started getting messages from Purdue, to make sure that the experiment was successful!" Nina reasoned, and Lydia's eyes betrayed her exact deduction too. "Now he had the perfect opportunity to reveal that you were still alive! Obviously the highest bidder would want to get your whereabouts from Healy and I think Sam just discovered who he gave it to."

Lydia looked at Nina with an ashen expression. She finally realized that she truly was in danger and she knew that at least four other people knew about the Tesla Experiment. Any of those could be showing up at her door at any moment.

"Nina, get that skinny ass of yours behind my chair and wheel me to the second floor! Now! We have some time to prepare to dig in here at the chamber in case Purdue makes contact, so let's make it count!"

CHAPTER 27

*T*he entire region of Haute-Vienne suffered a night of tense anticipation as the dreadful news spread through the small towns. Oradour-sur-Glane reeked of burning flesh, ammunition and scorched agricultural produce stored in barns that were now reduced to ash. The German regiment responsible decided to stay for the night to enjoy the spoils of their exploits, but the commanders did elect to send out scouts to comb the surrounding farms and communes to flush out whomever could be holding Kämpfe.

Being wounded by a falling beam under one of the structures earlier had Sturmbannführer Diekmann incapacitated. The medical officer had administered morphine to still his pain, putting him to sleep for the night. Purdue used the opportunity to slip away behind the back of the only structure that was practically ignored, save for being used as sleeping quarters for the night. The young girl had followed Purdue's advice reluctantly, but she knew that any man who killed one of the Germans to save her had to be someone she could trust. She had no choice otherwise.

The clumps of pea brushes populated most of the next

kilometer of land off the boundary of the obliterated town. There were trees and the odd brook running through the terrain which was pivotal to her survival, and she found a place by the water to hide until morning. Her body was weary, exhausted from the emotional devastation of what had happened to the people she knew so well but the water soothed her skin and burning eyes in the coolness of night.

She heard a rustling somewhere in the pea brushes. The fair haired man from earlier was stumbling through the dense foliage, having no idea where he was going. It was good to see him, yet she was afraid to show herself. He collapsed to his knees in the water, gulping up handfuls of it and washing his face. For a long while he just sat there in the faint light of the moon while she scrutinized him.

"You are English?" she said hesitantly from her hiding place.

Purdue perked up. He was not sure if he heard what he thought he did, so he just listened. "Are you hurt?" she said again.

"Where are you?" he gasped. "I am from Scotland, yes. Your English is good."

She stood up, drawing Purdue's attention. "Merci."

He waded through the uneven growth of bushes to her side and whispered, "I hope your family was not there in that town."

"My family is dead. Long ago. But those people were like family," she cried. Her small hands covered her eyes as her body shook, making Purdue feel a hundred times worse about bringing Diekmann and his devils here.

"I'm so very sorry. They were looking for one of their commanders and we thought he was here," Purdue explained in the most tender voice he could manage. They sat in the silence of the wildness outside the two that was still alight with tormenting fires.

"That man you are looking for is in *Oradour-sur-Veyres*," she mentioned matter-of-factly, playing in the ground with a stick she picked up to defend herself with before.

Purdue sighed, "Yes, we know that now. But now it is too late for your town."

"So if you let them find him all this death would be for nothing," she speculated, impressing Purdue with her mature sensibilities. "Are you going to lead them there to kill those people too?"

Her words shocked Purdue to the core. At first he wanted to retort, but he realized that she was absolutely correct. He would cause another massacre if he allowed Diekmann to know where Kämpfe *really* was. Nina had the right information, Lydia gave him the right information and he went and gave the wrong details. It was all his fault and he had to make up for it. In his mind he figured that he could still procure the Tesla schematics from Helmut if he could find his way to Oradour-sur-Veyres.

"No, I am fleeing from them too," he said. "My name is Dave. And I am going to make sure the same fate does not fall to the next town."

"I'm Celeste," she said. "If you want to warn them, we should go now in the night, Dave. I want to get as far from Oradour as I can! Please."

"So do I, young Celeste, so do I," Purdue said firmly. "But how will we get there?"

"Come," she said, and got up. "We have to get to Henri's farm. He can take us to the town if we tell him what it is about."

"Who is Henri?" he asked her.

"A farmer we know well. His son is one of my friends and he is in touch with the Resistance. I will not tell them that you came with the intruders otherwise they might arrest or kill you," Celeste said.

"That is a good point. The prisoner they have there has something of mine that I want back," Purdue lied, but if Helmut was anything like the animals he was to be rescued by, there was no reason to feel sorry for him.

Purdue and Celeste stalked through the trees and along the rocks, keeping out of the moonlight most of the time. In his mind Purdue was very worried about reporting to Lydia and with the night overhead it was a constant reminder that his days in this point of the tapestry had come to an end. As long as he could collect the schematics soon he could get to a place where he could use the BAT, hopefully to return home.

"Come, over here," Celeste whispered, jerking at Purdue's sleeve. "There, down there, see?" He looked down on the shallow valley and saw two small structures in the trees where a yellow glow emanated through the windows. On approach they heard that the farm's people were outside, talking with someone else.

"It looks like Joseph Jean is there too," Celeste whispered as she ducked through the trees, leading Purdue along in the shadows of the trees.

"Who is he?" he asked her.

"The leader of the local militia," she revealed. "He will definitely be able to take you to the German officer.

Purdue was nervous. If word came out that he came with Diekmann's unit he would be done for. There was no way of telling how the farmers would construe the arrival of a stranger from nowhere accompanying a child from the town the Nazi's had just decimated and razed utterly. His French was good enough to understand the people in front of the house, but he told Celeste that he would prefer she translate for them when needed.

"Who's there?" Henri shouted into the dark trees as Celeste and Purdue came down the small winding path. He aimed with his shotgun into the dark, joined shortly after by

Joseph. Both men had their barrels pointing right at the two
figures they discerned in the shadows.

"Don't shoot! Don't shoot, Henri!" Celeste cried. "Raise
your hands, Dave," she told her companion. Her voice was
shaky.

At such a young age the poor girl had not just had to
endure the death of her parents years ago but now she had
lost her only home and the only people she still had to
protect her. Her flight thus far had kept her calm from neces-
sity, to help the English stranger and to stay alive in the grasp
of the Nazi's, but the girl was still in shock from the attack
and from what she had to witness. Trauma was edging away
at her nerves and her vulnerable psyche, but she had to get to
safety first, before she could start to process what had
happened to her.

"Celeste?" Henri frowned. "Marie! Marie, it is Celeste!
She is alive!" He aced to swoop up the girl in a tight embrace,
but Purdue kept his gesture of surrender while the other
man held him up with the gun.

For the first time Celeste allowed herself to cry again.
Henri's wife, Marie, came out with a shawl to cover the girl.
She embraced Celeste and consoled her as she broke down.

"Sit down by the fire," Henri told Purdue as they pushed
him into the small house.

Celeste recovered long enough to speak again. "This is
Dave. He saved me from the Nazi's and he is looking for the
prisoner you have, Jean. Can you help us?"

Jean and Henri stared at Purdue, and then exchanged
astonished glances between them. The whole house went
quiet and even Henri's wife let go of Celeste for a moment to
look at Purdue. In the firelight they could now see him properly and their faces froze in suspicion, and an inkling of fear.

"What do you want with the prisoner?" Jean asked

Purdue, breaking the spell they all seemed to have fallen under for a second.

"He has papers, designs, of a very dangerous weapon the Nazi's want to use to kill their enemies in their masses. I was sent to make sure he does not get those papers back to the Germans," Purdue explained, using some dramatic license to enhance his story and look better in their eyes. He reckoned that telling them how their friends were tortured and killed because of him might bring him some disadvantage. It was imperative that the French Resistance see him as an ally.

"Are you related to him?" Henri asked.

"No, not at all. Why?" Purdue asked in alarm. He did not need to be affiliated with Helmut Kämpfe at all, especially among these people.

"Bring Dave some water, please. You have never met him before, the captive?" Henri asked as his wife got Purdue something to drink.

"No, never. That is why Celeste suggested I ask for Jean to take me to him. I have no idea what he looks like," Purdue admitted, gratefully accepting the cool water from Marie.

The men scoffed, even smiled a little.

"We'll take you to him in the early morning," Jean agreed finally. Purdue had no choice but to trust them. For now he had to get some rest and hope that Diekmann would not send emissaries looking for him before he got to Kämpfe. More than that, he was terribly worried about the BAT and its rapidly withering power.

CHAPTER 28

*J*n the very early hours, while they were all asleep, Purdue slipped into the stables outside to report to Lydia and let her know that he was planning to come back. The box lit up, but the power was considerably less this time, hardly out-shining the interior of the empty stables. Still, he spoke into the microphone.

"Hope you can hear me?" he started. "Please ready the chamber. I intend to return in…" he checked the watch he took from the dead Nazi he left at the horse cart, set to the original entry time, "…twelve hours exactly."

A crackle grew louder and the frequency hummed as he waited with baited breath. There was a weak signal sound, then a voice.

"—ave, Nina says— Helmut…—ds the Tes— papers where no-one can take it from him!' Lydia shouted. He could hear Nina directing her in the background.

"What does that mean?" he asked.

'Pur—, you cannot — back yet. We have trouble here…" Nina tried to tell him, but he had no idea what they were talking about.

"Where is Sam? Nina? Nina!"

Before he could continue the light waned and the box was left far cooler than it used to be when he was done transmitting – not steaming like a blacksmith's iron anymore, but hardly smoldering.

He collected the BAT and slipped it back into his pocket. He checked the time again, just to make sure he knew where twelve hours would take him. There was no more time to waste. He deliberately made a ruckus in washing up in the outside trough so that his guide would wake up.

"If you don't mind," Purdue told Jean, "I have urgent business with your prisoner."

A half hour later Jean and Purdue bade the farmer, Marie and young Celeste goodbye and made the trip to Oradour-sur-Veyres. On the way there Jean hardly spoke a word to the English stranger, but he certainly looked at him a lot.

"What are you going to do with the papers you want from the Nazi officer, then?" he asked. Purdue had to sift through the right phrases to keep up his reputation as a friend while not mentioning anything far-fetched that could alienate Jean and his movement. The French Resistance could not find out that he was a guest of the Reichkanzlei or that he showed up from thin air, so to speak.

"My organization will destroy it after committing it to record for historical documentation," Purdue employed his tact. He felt like an attorney or a publicist, spinning the truth to twist it into something acceptable. Among all the questions he did his best to answer, Purdue was dying to ask one of his own. He desperately wanted to know why they studied him so, why they could not stop staring at him. He hoped that they did not by chance see him with Diekmann's company and now recognized him.

"If you don't mind I will accompany you when you go to see the German officer," Jean finally said. "That is our only condition for you to be allowed to see him. And only because you saved our Celeste. Just know that."

"I am grateful for the opportunity, Jean. Believe me, I completely understand that you will not allow a stranger to speak to your prisoner. I have no problem with that," Purdue smiled respectfully, yet inside he dreaded the notion. He needed to be left alone with Helmut Kämpfe to attain the papers, but if this was the only way to get near him, it would have to suffice.

Just after 10am in the morning they arrived on the hill above the small town of Oradour-sur-Vayres. Purdue's stomach churned. He had never before felt such a feeling of foreboding from all sides as he did now. Not only was he running out of time with the BAT, but he had to remember that by now, Diekmann had to be aware that he absconded. With German scouts all about the Haute-Vienne department keeping an eye out for him, he could not move about freely without taking note of prying glares in is direction.

"Let me do all the talking, Dave," Jean told him as they drove into town. "I will make sure they don't overreact to your presence. This is a very sensitive matter, especially now that the Nazi's destroyed one of our towns in retaliation for this man's capture. In fact, most men here are just waiting to kill the pig."

"I don't blame them," Purdue answered inadvertently, but his words pleased Jean.

He gave Purdue a hat to conceal his hair and face and told him that it was so that Diekmann's men would not see him here, but in truth Jean was hiding Purdue's looks for quite another reason. "Come, Dave. Let's get this over with."

After the men of the Resistance were briefed on who Purdue was and what he did for Celeste he was reluctantly allowed to go into the small shack hidden behind the water mill where they were keeping the Nazi officer. Following

THE TESLA EXPERIMENT

Jean and his shotgun into the musty little room decked out with nothing more than a few heaps of straw and a bucket for waste. The Resistance was definitely not kind captors to any Nazi.

"There he is," Jean said, pointing to the crouched up officer. He was barefoot, his German uniform stripped off with only a dirty vest on his torso. His head was bowed over his folded arms and his legs pulled up.

"Achtung!" Jean mocked him. "You have a visitor!"

The officer did not bother to respond at first, but Purdue stepped forward and said, "Helmut, I bring greetings from Lydia Jenner." The officer immediately caught his breath and lifted his face to see the man who could achieve the impossible. Jean waited for both reactions, knowing that they would see one another as if in a mirror. Just as Nina had a double in Sigrun, Purdue had the same face and hair as Helmut!

"What in God's name?" he marveled at the sight of the Nazi officer. In turn Helmut looked absolutely spooked. Helmut rose to his shackled feet with much effort, but he had to. What he saw before him was unbelievable. He stared at Purdue for a moment and then he smiled, "No wonder Lydia Jenner wanted to sleep with me. I look just like the man she had been in love with since college!" He burst out in laughter. Jean raised his gun in defense, not used to the boisterous behavior of the normally quiet prisoner.

"You didn't know?" he laughed. "She told me all about you, Dave Purdue!"

"What did she tell you?" Purdue shouted, unsettled by his recognition. Jean had no idea what was happening.

"You were the one she loved since she met you. She told me that I reminded her of you, but you know what? It was still *my* name she screamed!" he sniggered in amusement, winking at Purdue. "Now you are here? She sent you, of all

189

people, back to get the Tesla papers from me? How terribly vindictive!"

"You have the papers with you?" Purdue asked, electing to ignore the hostility seeping from Helmut's words.

"Nein."

"Where are they?" he asked Helmut.

"Burned. I pinned them to a Jew in Limoges and watched Tesla's genius go up in flames with him," he said nonchalantly. Jean pursed his lips and played with his finger on the trigger. "Tell the French dog to shoot me, then, Dave Purdue!"

Purdue and Jean exchanged glances. They both desired the end of the Nazi. Purdue knew that Helmut would not have gone through the trouble of obtaining Nikola Tesla's documents all the way from the United States if he did not plan to sell them or use them for the good of the Reich.

"Strip him," Purdue ordered.

"What?" Jean frowned.

"Strip the Nazi swine," Purdue repeated, switching his innate jovial nature for one far darker to accommodate the handling of a reprehensible character such as Helmut. "The schematic I am looking for is on him and I want it."

Jean summoned his men and against the prisoner's struggling they stripped him of every grain of clothing he wore. Nude, he stood there screaming at them in German, but they stood mute and fascinated at what they saw. On his back and stomach the precise design details of Nikola Tesla's *Teleforce* weapon was tattooed, complete with notes.

"Jean, in Berlin there is a secret society, the Vril Society, led by two females. They are affiliated with Hitler and they intend to use this design to create a weapon that will wipe out entire armies and air forces at a time," Purdue told the leader of the Resistance. "If this officer is rescued by the Nazi's who are on their way here now, he will deliver the weapon's design to them and then Germany will have the power to overthrow the whole world."

Jean got the message. Without hesitation he shot Helmut in the head.

"Skin him!" he shouted to his men. "Peel that design from his carcass and prepare it for our friend here to take with him. Dave, we have to avert the Nazi's on their way here. Are you with us?"

"Hell yes," Purdue smiled. "We have to destroy the 2nd Panzer Division before they pass Saint-Auvent and I need you to contact your associates in Berlin to let them know where to find Maria Orschitsch and her associate, Sigrun. Once you have them, the mass destruction the Third Reich could inflict will be neutralized."

CHAPTER 29

$\mathcal{N}$ina and Lydia were wide awake by sheer fear and worry. Neither had slept in over a day and now that Sam was absent and Purdue was almost due back they could not afford a moment's distraction.

"You are officially one of my favorite inventors, Professor Jenner," Nina remarked.

"Why, thank you, Dr. Gould," Lydia grinned.

They each sat in their places next to the *Voyager III,* armed to the teeth. Lydia had introduced Nina to her storeroom where she kept all her inventions, those not pertaining to particle acceleration or Einstein's theories. During her stint with the SAS as advisor, where she met Healy, Lydia had a fascination with munitions. In effect, the sheeting all around her house and inside was not just to regulate the decibels her sensitive senses were influenced with.

Lydia used it to make a tank of her house. Reinforced steel was in place to protect her should there be an outbreak of war. Healy used to tell her that she was paranoid, but little did he know that she was preparing to defend her home against those who would come to end her life for her secrets.

It was another devastating fact she discovered while working on the Tesla Experiment.

"It is the reason why I deliberately made sure that only I kept the data on the progress of the experiment," she told Nina while they sat in the dead silence, having a smoke. "I quickly noticed that my colleagues and my investors took too much an interest in taking over the experiment once I started showing positive progress."

"Jesus. So they don't know you came back, and still they have been searching for the data?" Nina asked.

"Correct. Thinking me dead, they started snooping around CERN, hoping to find lost information. They employed Tägtgren to keep an eye, they…"

"*'They'* being who?" Nina interrupted eagerly.

"The Cornwall Institute. They supplied a lot of the funding, but once I disappeared they kept watch over the experiment's legacy, just in case something surfaced," Lydia explained, her eyes scanning the markings on the weapon she had in front of her on the table.

"And when Sam showed up on the CCTV at the Alice, all hell broke loose," Nina remarked. "Now I get it. By that time Purdue was already here with you?"

"Yes, I never stopped experimenting, you see," Lydia disclosed, having no idea that Nina was recording everything she said for Sam's sake, should he need the evidence. Lydia was spilling her heart now, looking utterly worn by it all. But she was tranquil for once, as if Nina managed to calm her by accepting all her reasons without prejudice.

"I kept trying to get back to Helmut to get Tesla's work he stole, but my body was just too frail. That was why I finally summoned Dave in desperation. I knew he would understand. But I did not mean to involve so many people in my little secret success," she said through the smoke she exhaled. "Just Purdue. He deserved the glory, you know?"

Lydia chuckled sorrowfully, knowing she would never have him, especially now.

"I loved him. I still do. You know what that is like," she told Nina.

Nina nodded. More and more it became evident that Lydia was not planning to resurface. She planned to stay dead, to be dead. And when the time came she wanted Purdue, the man she loved secretly, to take the credit for her inventions.

"I wanted to give him the acclaim that he deserved in this world, in this era, you see? I wanted Dave Purdue to be my Tesla," she smiled at Nina with a shimmer in her eyes.

Nina smiled sweetly at the professor. Now that she understood what the whole experiment was really about she would do everything to help accomplish Lydia's endgame.

"I am sorry, Lydia, for being such a bitch," Nina apologized. "I had no idea what was really going on."

"Look, I know why you went off at me, but I could not let you in on all the secrets yet, could I? I had to leave you to believe that I was some power hungry bitch who did not care what happened to Purdue, even while I was shattered to know that he may never make it back on my account. But now I am very glad I got you to understand the method to my madness...and God, am I full of madness!" she laughed. "I just really hope that we can get him back and if we do, that he does not sustain this amount of damage."

"Do you think his body would hold out?" Nina asked. "I mean, did you calculate his time there to accommodate..."

Lydia gave her a look of reprimand.

"Of course you did. Just checking," Nina smiled.

"If his return voyage goes smoothly, he should be fine, physically. My damage came solely from miscalculating the difference in duration. I only have one concern," Lydia sighed. "If the voltage of the BAT is too low the device in his mouth will not be able to amplify the frequencies – the various fields at play – enough. That sound wave emitted by the radio signal is almost more important than the electrical current itself."

Nina gave it some thought. "You know, I am not one for this scientific stuff, but would it help to use an amplifier of sorts? Maybe turn up the volume on the radio pulse at the moment of the voyage?"

"That would work, but the problem is that this kind of sound we need would certainly blow up my damn head! My ears cannot handle that kind of emission," Lydia explained.

Nina looked at the control board with all its copper wiring, old screens and large dials. She had no idea what was going on there, but she would do anything to help Lydia get Purdue back successfully. She leaned forward and looked at Lydia. "Do you trust me?"

"Now why would you say that?" Lydia moaned, putting out her cigarette.

"If you tell me what to do, I'll do it on your behalf when the time comes. You can close yourself up in one of your soundproof rooms and I will bring him back," Nina said.

"You are serious, aren't you?" Lydia smiled at the brave historian.

"Aye."

"Get me a piece of paper and a pencil," Lydia said with renewed hope. "He should be checking in for the voyage back in about 15 minutes, so we had better hurry."

CHAPTER 30

*P*rofessor Westdijk kept looking in his rear view mirror.

"Listen, Sam, where are we going?" he asked.

Sam did not want to relay all the madness of the experiment to the professor for fear that the old man would not believe him.

"It is a long story, professor, but I promise I will fill you in as soon as we are safely inside the property and get rid of this maniac," he told the old man at the wheel. "For what it is worth, you would find it fascinating."

"Well, I'll say this...you don't have a boring life, my boy," Professor Westdijk replied, changing lanes again to keep their pursuer from catching up. "You will have to give me an address, or else I am not going to know where to go!"

Foster was right on top of them, occasionally slowing down enough not to draw too much attention. But he had the eyes of a hawk, never losing them ahead of him. Along the Rhône they sped towards Jenner Manor. Sam punched the address into the GPS while watching the speeding red vehicle in their wake, keeping up with them every step of the way.

"Sam, if I am risking my life to help you, the least you can do is tell me where we are going," Professor Westdijk implored and he wove the car through traffic.

"A friend of mine asked me to stay and help him and an old university colleague with an experiment. That is all. Remember when I first met you?" Sam asked.

"Yes, at the hotel and at CERN," the old man affirmed.

"The interview I conducted with the engineer?" Sam asked again.

"Yes?"

"He was murdered and they think it was me," Sam disclosed. Westdijk looked at him with wide eyes, but said nothing. "I didn't do it, I swear to God!"

"So this chase is to get away from the Cornwall people?" he asked Sam.

"Aye. We have to get to Lydia's house before he catches up with us, because I think I have done enough to stretch their patience. They are aiming to kill me this time," Sam said, turning again to look behind him.

They turned into the last street, shedding most of the traffic to only match speed and wits with Foster as they raced to make it to Jenner Manor. Sam called Nina, but the signal was too weak. The rain was pouring on the road, forcing Prof. Westdijk to slow down around the corners. Foster came so close that Sam could look him in the eye.

"Honk the horn. God, the place is soundproof!" Sam recalled to his dismay. But he underestimated Nina. Knowing that her cell phone signal would be perturbed and that she would not hear them coming, she stood on the balcony outside her guest room.

"Here they come, Lydia!" she shouted down to the lobby, where the hostess waited for her alert. From there she opened the gates for Sam and Prof. Westdijk to come roaring into the yard. Unfortunately the gates did not close as quickly as they needed.

As they raced through the gate Foster pushed down the accelerator pedal of his car and crossed the gateway just as the steel plated gates slid shut. The edge of the gate caught the rear brake light and bumper as it closed, but he made it through.

In the pouring rain Sam and the professor rushed for the back door. The low branches of the backyard would make it difficult for Foster to move fast. With the gate shut the doors to the mansion was unlocked until Sam was inside.

"Nina! Where are you?" he shouted.

"Chamber! Hurry, so Lydia can lock the door to the basement area!" Nina cried from down the hall.

"Come, Professor! We have to go downstairs. It is safe there for now," Sam said, dragging the confused old man with him. As they descended the ramp toward the underground area where the ladies waited, they could hear gunshots outside the kitchen. Foster used his colossal frame to ram the door after shooting the electronic locks.

Sam and Prof. Westdijk rushed in and Nina shut the door.

"Thank God you're safe!" she panted, flinging her arms around Sam in a passionate embrace. He was soaking wet and his body was shivering from more than the cold. The nerve wrecking encounter he had endured since he was abducted had his body shaking uncontrollably. "Oh, Sam, I was so worried that you would never come back," Nina said, looking deep into his dark eyes. He kissed her with the same affection she showed him, not wanting to let he go this time.

"I don't mean to break up this happy union," Prof. Westdijk said, "but there is a man trying to kill us."

"He won't get in here," Nina said confidently. "This door

in enforced steel with an electrical current running through it."

"Nina! Nina! He has made contact! Come!" Lydia shouted frantically, summoning Nina to the control board.

"Purdue," Nina smiled at Sam's befuddled expression. "Purdue is about to come back through! Come!"

Sam followed Nina as the loud crackle started. Lydia had disappeared into the small soundproof room to avoid the amplified sound frequency from killing her. Sam watched Nina handle the board like an expert scientist. One by one she turned the four *field knobs* to exactly the frequency and voltage directed on the paper Lydia drew for her. Sam took up his recorder to get footage of the process. As the crackle increased in sound, and the entry time neared, the power failed.

"Oh sweet Jesus! No!" Nina screamed, bashing her fists on the table next to her. It was pitch dark.

"It's not the weather," Sam voice came through the darkness. "Foster tripped the power from the kitchen, the son of a bitch!"

Lydia opened the door to ascertain what had happened. Distraught, she cursed furiously. "What the fuck is happening? Why now?"

"Don't worry, we'll get him back as soon as we get rid of Foster," Sam reached for the battery powered spare lights under the wall desk while Nina and Lydia collectively fumed at the failure to bring Purdue back.

"Who is Foster?" Lydia asked.

"A mercenary the Cornwall Institute hired to kill me, because they think I killed the CERN engineer that witnessed your little trip back in time, Lydia," Sam explained while switching on the lights one by one. They were faint, but adequate for them to check the breakers, at least.

A thunderous din echoed from the door as Foster tried to fight his way through.

"Open the door, Sam! I just want to speak to you!" Foster shouted.

"Aye, of course you do!" Sam hollered back through the door. Without the electrical currents running along the steel plating the house was not half as secure as before.

"Christ!" Lydia screamed. "Not you!"

Sam and Nina turned to see Westdijk aim a weapon at Lydia.

"Professor! She is not the enemy!" Sam exclaimed harshly. "Our problem is on the other side of this door!"

"Hello Professor Jenner," he greeted Lydia with the hiss of a snake. "Holding out on us, are you?"

"Sam, open that goddamn door!" Lydia screamed.

"No way!" he refused, but Nina knew to trust Lydia's judgment.

She lunged past Sam and unbolted the door, and Foster burst through. Sam tried to stop him, but he knocked the journalist off his feet with one jab. Westdijk cocked his weapon, holding it steady on Lydia.

"Go and switch on the power!" he insisted. "I want to see what comes through the ether this time. And here we thought the Tesla Experiment did not work. Switch the power on," he spelled it out for Nina. Nina shook her head and moved in behind Foster.

Professor Westdijk lost his patience. He turned the gun toward Nina and shot Foster in his tracks. He fell at Nina's feet, exposing her to the gun. Hysterically she screamed and crouched down next to Sam, holding him. "Sam, wake up!" Another shot rang just short of them, evoking another scream from her.

"Go and switch on the power or I will kill everyone in this house," he roared. "I have spent enough time and money trying to bring the Tesla Experiment into fruition and here you go behind my back, Lydia?"

"You wanted this experiment to work so that you could build the death ray, and that is as far as your loyalty towards science stretched, you money grabbing charlatan!" Lydia growled at him.

"That's why this big monster tripped the power?" Nina asked.

"To prevent Purdue from coming through with the schematic. So that this piece of shit would not get his hands on it!" Lydia ranted. "He would build the *teleforce* weapon so that he could become the master of war, bringing the governments of the world to their knees with its undeniably destructive reach."

"Why else, Lydia?" Westdijk asked. "Why else would you create something so brilliant and not use it to keep the world's terrorists in check?"

"Because it would mean that you are just another terrorist, imposing your will on others by means of tyranny, you idiot!" she seethed. "But you don't care. As long as you end up stinking rich and exempt, you don't care where the weapon ends up."

"Well, whatever you tried to do is down the drain now, pal," Nina said. "The time window for Purdue to come back through has passed. You will never have the design now."

Sam opened his eyes. With a motion of his head he directed her to the video camera he left on the desk from where he gathered up the battery powered lights. Nina smiled. No matter what happened next, there would be proof on camera of the professor's involvement in the web of deceit surrounding the CERN fire incident.

"That remains to be seen, my dear girl," he told Nina. "I can always call Penny Richards and tell her that Sam Cleave killed Christian Foster too."

"Go ahead," Sam said. "We'll implicate her too. After all, Tägtgren was working for both you and her. I am sure she would love to know that her dear friend, the professor, was the one trying to sabotage all the experiments conducted by the Cornwall Institute all along."

"Now it seems we have a problem," Professor Westdijk said calmly. "I will not leave until you bring your associate back with my schematic. And it is no use you all getting killed for nothing, is it?"

"It is too late," Lydia lamented. "His energy would have bonded to the point where he is now, so there is no way to come back anymore."

"Oh my God, Lydia. For a genius you really possess a very restricted mind!" Professor Westdijk shrieked in exasperation. He paced around the chamber she had built, but kept the gun on her. "You are going to get this contraption up and running. And Sam Cleave will be your..." he smiled, "... voyager. Just because your other friend is a thing of the past, doesn't mean we cannot follow up. Let him go get it for us, while I make sure we can bring him back safely, right?"

Sam and Nina looked at Lydia. She did not move for a long while, before finally letting out a deep sigh. "I suppose there is nothing else we can do," she shrugged. "Purdue was an unfortunate casualty, but we did all we could do."

"There is no fucking way I am getting in that oven of yours, Professor Jenner. You can shoot me first!" Sam protested.

"I'll shoot your girlfriend," Westdijk smiled, "if you don't go, Sam. Easy as that."

CHAPTER 31

*P*urdue was devastated that he could not make contact long enough with Lydia and Nina on the other side of his transmission. To make matters worse he could not discuss his predicament with anyone here. They would either think he was insane, as Diekmann did, or they would laugh it off as a joke. Hopeless, he sat on the bank of the small rivulet a few meters from Jean's house. After the French Resistance sent out their scouts to stop the advancing convoys Purdue was welcome to spend some time relaxing at the little stream.

Jean had noticed how troubled the English stranger seemed, but he did not want to impose. Purdue wanted some solitude to think about a way to get in touch with Lydia and Nina even if it was too late for him to return. From his right pocket he pulled the BAT, now virtually worthless to him. He just shook his head, unable to formulate a way to get it to work again.

"What are you doing?" a voice asked behind him. It was Celeste. She had come with Henri and his family to find protection in the mountains.

"I'm just thinking," he smiled sadly.

"What is that?" she asked.

"Just a little radio device I can't use anymore," Purdue explained, trying to stay positive and kind while his world was falling apart inside him.

"Why? Are the batteries flat?" she asked.

He looked up at her, surprised at the simple way in which children saw conundrums. He nodded and tossed it up a few times, catching it again.

"So why don't you charge the batteries again?" she asked.

"How?" Purdue played along, not giving her solution a second thought.

"Jean and his brother use the water wheels here to generate electricity," she mentioned casually. "You should ask them to help you charge the batteries for you."

Purdue could not believe it. Her common observation was actually quite solid. Instantly his own heart felt recharged too. He jumped up and dusted off his clothes.

"Celeste, could you show me where they generate the electricity?" he asked.

"Of course," she smiled. "Come, I'll show you."

She walked up past the water mill and pointed out a small stone building, no bigger than Purdue's bathroom back home. Inside he could only marvel at what he found. There were a myriad of devices and dials connected to various conductors that ran along the walls. The water wheel acted as generator for the four small houses outside town, so that they could be independent of the rest of the commune. Purdue was elated.

"Dear Celeste, you have no idea how clever you are!" he cheered with a warm smile. The girl did not know what was so amazing about what she suggested, but she was happy for Purdue nonetheless. He went to see Jean to ask his permission to use his generator. Of course Jean wanted to know what he needed it for, and with a grown up the battery explanation would not be sufficient.

"I have to charge this device to a certain amount of volts, Jean. And unfortunately it is a matter of urgency. My time is running out to…" he gave it some thought, "…contact the people who sent me by using this radio. But the charge has run out and I need it to communicate."

"Oh, that should be very easy," the Frenchman replied. "Why didn't you just say so?"

Purdue hoped that he could have the device charged to the required voltage to reach the right thermal point, otherwise his attempts would be futile. Jean leaned against the wall of the small shack, "So what do you use this device for?"

It was the question Purdue had dreaded. He had no idea how Jean would take it if he had to tell him the truth.

"I need it to be charged so high that it would be able to reach a certain temperature when I switch it on," Purdue explained, trying to sound as serious as possible. But to his pleasant surprise his host did not care for much more than that.

"Oh, alright then. Connect it up and charge it as long as you think. I have to meet with some of the militia members in a few minutes. Would you excuse me?" he asked cordially.

"Absolutely," Purdue smiled. "Don't let me keep you."

He would let the BAT charge for the next few hours and attempt contact soon after. It worried him that they claimed to have trouble on the other side. It made him feel helpless, but as soon as he had juiced up the BAT he would find out what was going on. Not only did he need to contact Lydia, but he had to get the word out to allies of the French Resistance.

Purdue did not want to imperil the people of the French countryside with his presence there, but he could not let them know that he was the reason the Nazi's were scouring

the small towns. With Helmut dead and the macabre keep-
sake in Purdue's possession, it was time to leave them behind
so that he could transmit to Lydia and hopefully return home
this time. With the BAT in his pocket he hitched a ride with
one of Jean's men, making his way back up toward where he
knew Diekmann's division would be stationed for the next
few days. He alerted the local militia and told them where to
ambush the 2nd Panzer Division 'Das Reich' before the
Allieds locked on to the Vril Society under the noses of
the SS.

In Berlin the clandestine societies that represented the
Allied Forces, even various operatives and celebrities from
the United Kingdom and the United States gathered their
resources to create a dragnet for the Vril Society's leaders.
Masquerading as interested parties versed in the occult,
psychics and mediums from all over Germany sought out the
two women who led the Vril Society.

Purdue knew that he had to find a way to get back to
Lyon, 2015 at all costs. With the French Resistance at his
side, he managed to spread the word about the Vril's plans to
reinforce the Reich's weapons with Tesla's work and use
their power to topple the Nazi's. Hitler was furious.

In Berlin the Nazi High Command had ordered the arrest
of all the members of the Vril Society and the Black Sun.
This was, however, not what was written in history books,
the reason for which would also explain the discrepancies
between historical facts and what Purdue found to be
happening first hand. But he was not to realize this just yet.

What baffled him was the fact that he ran into doppel-
gangers almost everywhere he went. Several people he met
along the way were the spitting image of people he knew in
his place and time. Famous people from history turned out

to look quite different from those he had learned of in his history text books and so even the dates of certain events differed slightly. He wrote it off to inaccurate accounts or the manipulation of information.

Purdue made the rest of his journey on foot to avoid being detected by German forces in France. Outside one of the small villages he hiked up through the woods. Just before his twelve hours had run out, he slipped into a low hanging cliff that formed a cave structure, and he got ready one last time to return home.

CHAPTER 32

$\mathcal{L}$ ydia was no longer the target of the greedy professor. Now he had Nina sitting right in front of him, threatening Sam with her life if he did not carry out his order.

"You know, Sam, if he shoots me he is still not going to get what he wants," Nina said defiantly.

"Would you like to call that bluff, madam?" Westdijk asked, sitting back on the chair opposite the table from Nina.

"Don't rock the boat, Nina," Lydia said softly. She was at the control desk, ready to heat up the Voyager III for Sam's unfortunate departure to join Purdue at the same so-called coordinates. "He is a psycho of the highest order who would do anything for a bit of money."

Sam was busy getting dressed in the same kind of protective gear Purdue was wearing when he successfully went through the ether. He procrastinated, hoping that Purdue would make contact one more time. Surely the event would distract Westdijk long enough for Sam to overwhelm him, but Purdue was a no-show, as they feared.

"You do know that this is a ludicrous attempt, right?"

Lydia told Westdijk. "The machine moves like a line of cars in a one way street. We sent someone down and we cannot send another down until the other has come back up…not without resetting everything."

"Then reset it," he sneered at her.

Nina was livid. She hated feeling so helpless. Here they were being bullied by one person, when there were two of them who could attack him if he could only be distracted long enough. She was disappointed that the weapons she and Lydia had at their disposal before were now mere ornaments cast aside on the wall desk.

The only solace was the running video camera. It was Nina's biggest flaw, in her own opinion, that she could never accept when she was in a corner. While so many ideas for possible solutions went fleeting through her mind, Lydia was devising a plan of her own.

"Come on, my boy! Not even a woman takes that long to get dressed!" Prof. Westdijk shouted to Sam.

Nina's eyes wandered toward the weapons on the desk, but Lydia's expression suggested she abandon the notion for now. On the screen Nina saw Lydia punch in a code that was not there before, one to short circuit the machine. Westdijk would not know the difference, never having seen this kind of chamber before. Sam still ran the risk of being electrocuted, even without being caught in the middle of the unified fields and that is what Lydia was most concerned about.

"Will Purdue never come back again?" Nina asked out of the blue to procrastinate.

"I don't think so. Not anymore," Lydia replied. "We would need considerable sound amplification to be carried along the electrical current at the same time that he attempts to come back and we lost that with the power failure."

From the far side of the hallway something stirred. It caught Nina's eye, but she did not pay attention to it. She did not want Prof. Westdijk to see that something was going on behind him. Suddenly the lights dipped and the screens flickered.

"What is that?" Westdijk shouted in suspicion.

"I don't know, probably the weather," Lydia replied, studying the lights against the ceiling. "We would have to keep the current strong if we want Sam to make it to the other side."

Through the speakers the strange electronic voice phenomenon sounded, starting Prof. Westdijk as it spoke next to him through the auxiliary monitors.

'—ia, charge now—home,' was all that came through. West-dijk jumped up to shoot Lydia. He looked completely ashen.

"Don't you dare switch it off!" he warned, but before he could pull the trigger Healy came at him from behind, striking him down.

"Dave! We don't have enough current to bring your back yet! Wait!" Lydia screamed back into the void. "He will be caught in the middle if we don't have enough sound to carry with the electricity, Nina!" she shouted in vain. Sam had no idea what to do, and neither did Nina. While Healy subdued Prof. Westdijk, Foster came stumbling from where he was shot. He looked at Lydia with determination in his eyes.

"Diamonds conduct sound, don't they?" he groaned.

Sam grabbed one of the guns and pointed to shoot.

"No!" Nina shouted. "Sam, don't shoot!"

Foster had his hand in his shirt. He ripped his diamond crucifix from his neck and flung it to Nina.

"Lydia, go to the soundproof room!" Nina yelled out as she positioned the diamond pendant to the power slot. She gave Lydia enough time to lock the door behind her so that the sonic clap would not kill her and then she shoved the diamond object into the hole like a wall plug, hoping that it would work.

Purdue was on his way back through the BAT's generator and from this side the diamond necklace increased the sound and thermal current of the machine to almost 1000 degrees Celsius, pulsing through the ether at a stronger rate than it had before. With a rush of lightning darting past them the chamber lit up with electricity, rapidly heating the atmosphere and roaring like thunder around them all. They cowered and took cover where they could as the pulse throbbed several times, threatening to bend the steel on the windows. Professor Westdijk looked up and rushed for a gun while the others were scattering. Purdue would not have a moment to collect himself before the professor would hold the gun on him to take Tesla's diagrams from him.

But as Purdue burst through the tapestry in the chamber a bolt of lightning radiated from the exterior of the chamber like the rays of the Black Sun. Westdijk was the only conductor standing up to receive the current. The blue cracks of electricity connected with him, attracted by the water in his cells and within a few seconds his body was charred beyond form under the onslaught of Tesla's famous coil.

Within moments of the mayhem all fell silent. Here and there a clap of a spark could be heard throughout the house. The majority of the electrical current was conducted by the steel plating along the walls of the house, lighting up all the lights in the entire manor and activating all the appliances at once. Healy was lying on his back, looking stunned. Lydia emerged from her soundproof room and helped Sam up. Under his body was Nina, safely shielded from any harm thanks to the journalist.

"Jesus Christ! Did you see that? We have managed to recreate the Tesla Coil!" Lydia shrieked with excitement.

Nina stood up slowly, holding on to Sam. He dusted off

her beautiful dark tresses and she fixed his shirt. She suddenly gasped, "Purdue! Where is Purdue?"

Sam and Healy opened the chamber door with much effort. Some of the rubber had melted onto the exterior metal, but inside they found Purdue lying curled up on the slant of the floor. His hair and eyebrows were singed off, but otherwise he was fine. His clothing was burned to shards in most places, leaving his reddened flesh exposed, but he did not suffer anything worse than a sunburn.

"Oh my God, Purdue! I'm so happy to see you!" Nina crooned ecstatically as the hugged him. The agony of her embrace woke the explorer. Purdue howled in pain.

"Sorry! Sorry!" Nina wailed, placing her hands over her mouth. "I forgot, Purdue, I'm so sorry!"

"Bring him out so I can see him," Lydia called from outside the chamber. The whole place was filled with smoke and the overwhelming stench of electrical fire. Nina smiled. She could hear Lydia's affection in her swift request. She wanted to see Purdue, not to ascertain if he successfully recovered the diagrams, but just to see him again. Healy and Sam helped the dazed Purdue from the heat of the Voyager III. Sam looked over at Healy, "You thought this would make amends for what you did?"

"No, I expect hell to rain on me, and rightly so, sir. But I am not sorry I came back," Healy replied. "Not even that lightning bolt could stop me from protecting Professor Jenner."

Sam was amazed that the butler still addressed him formally after all they had been through. Purdue slowly opened his eyes, moaning in pain. On the floor lay a heap of black ash that reeked up the place so badly that they wanted to vomit.

"Let's go to the drawing room, rather," Lydia suggested, and she did not have to invite them twice. Nina wheeled her up behind the men as they carried Purdue to the drawing room. Healy draped a cold cloth over Purdue's shoulders and they all sat down to recover from the frantic day they all had.

Exhausted, shocked, relieved; they sat in silence for a few minutes, just panting, coughing, groaning. Finally Healy went to fetch the Medical Kit to tend to Purdue's wounds for the time being until they would take him to hospital. Purdue stared at Nina across the room.

"What is the matter?" Sam asked.

"I met someone who looked precisely like Nina while I was captive in Hitler's bunker under the Reichkanzlei," Purdue smiled. "And Helmut…this is uncanny…"

"He looked just like you," Lydia recalled.

"That's right," Purdue winked at her, silently letting her know that he knew why she slept with Helmut while she was there. Lydia just shook her head and chuckled.

"What about Tesla's schematics?" Nina asked. "That is after all why you went, wasn't it?"

"I had it with me, but it was incinerated on the way back, I'm afraid," Purdue frowned. "I'm sorry, Lydia. It would appear that I failed you."

"No, sir. You did not!" she replied in her strong, forceful way. "After what I've seen today, I am bloody grateful we did not bring back the recipe to that ungodly invention. Can you imagine what the power hungry imbeciles would do with it? Poor Nina and Sam almost got killed over the *teleforce* weapon!"

"Well, now we know that time travel is possible," Sam announced.

"I would agree with you, Sam, had I not known that the formula I used had no principals of quantum physics," Lydia remarked.

"How do you mean? I was there," Purdue argued, "I was there in Nazi Germany in 1944. I had gone back in time."

"Not really," she contested. "You wondered by you saw so many famous people not looking the way we know them, right?"

"Yes," Purdue nodded.

"According to my own theory - based on Tesla, but largely augmented by myself," Lydia explained proudly, "you did not travel back in time, nor did you bend space. You actually punched through to another parallel universe. It is quite a different thing."

"Wait," Nina chipped in. "How? You mean Purdue went into another dimension?"

"No, darling. Another dimension is a different plane of existence that carries different frequencies to our physical existence. Purdue would have to be a ghost or a demon or an energy ball, whatever, to go there," Lydia gestured with her hands. "He was in a parallel universe, one just like ours with almost the same events and people. The difference is that this multi-verse is merely the product of different scenarios."

"So how this world would have been if things turned out differently?" Sam asked, trying to wrap his brain around the oddities of Lydia's ramblings.

"If Hitler never existed," she said abruptly, "one universe. If Mozart was a physician and not a musician – another universe...see where this is going?"

"My head hurts," Nina jested.

"This was why Dave saw people who looked like the exact twins of people here, just in a different life or environment," Lydia carried on. "The bottom line here is that we proved that we could punch through the veil of a parallel universe, where hopefully we could make a change to their history to keep them from making the same mistakes we made."

Purdue added, "Without having to worry about changing the future we now live in, as it would be with the past."

"That's it!" Lydia smiled. But unlike other times, she

seemed less flamboyant and loud about her experiments. To Purdue it seemed that his old friend was ready to hang up her gloves. He was happy for her to have gone out with a historical breakthrough, having no idea that she had passed over all achievements to his credit.

CHAPTER 33

"*T*his house brings back bad memories," Sam remarked. "Especially that bloody attic."

"Oh stop," Nina said, quickly closing the front door and locking it behind him. "I stay here alone and I'm still alive."

"Still, you are a very angry lady. Monsters won't even fuck with you," he reiterated. "I am however, bait for the denizens of the other realms."

"Come on, help me carry the last crate, please," she smiled. "I'll cook you dinner if you do."

It had been over three weeks since they left France and went their separate ways. But then Nina gave Sam a call to help her with some new acquisitions she needed to move into her house. Sam was delighted to see her again so soon. He even brought his cat, Bruichladdich, with him. As always, Bruich was on his own mission, seeking out the best spots to laze around in Nina's home in Oban.

"Have you heard from Purdue?" she asked Sam.

"Aye, he is still in Lyon with Lydia. They are compiling all their notes for a book about the Tesla Experiment and they want me to write the thing for them."

"Sounds like an interesting job," Nina replied. "What about Healy?"

"I decided not to press charges," Sam shrugged.

Nina could not believe it. "Are you daft? I'd let him have it!"

"Look, I did not get killed. And besides, I felt bad about luring Westdijk to Lydia…to all of you. It just goes to show that we all fuck up. And sometimes you mean well, you don't think that you are acting wrongfully and you end up putting others in danger," Sam explained in between groans of effort at the heavy crate.

"And all that time Foster was in fact after Westdijk. At least he perished while saving Purdue. I suppose that warrants some redemption, if you believe in that stuff," she smiled.

They carried the wooden crate toward the back of the house, where the winding steps that led up to the attic, had now been boarded up. "This goes in the back spare room, thank you."

"What is it?" Sam asked.

"Some old documents they found on a ship wreck off the coast of the Bering Straits. Belonged to some character from the Middle Ages, I think. Should make for some interesting reading, if I can decipher the writing," she rambled on.

"Who gave it to you?" Sam asked, hoping to rush her along so that she could keep that dinner promise.

"The University in Glasgow," Nina replied. "They discovered this through some salvagers who donated it. They want me to figure out what it is and assemble an index of sorts to have it exhibited at some point."

Sam waited until they had sat the big wooden box down.

"Shall I get us some pizza?" he asked.

Nina leered at him, annoyed that he could not wait for

her to cook something. "What is wrong with my cooking?" she asked with her hand in her side and one eyebrow raised.

"Nothing," he said softly. "But it's just that your kitchen freaks me out."

"Oh, Sam!" she snapped. "Get over it!"

They left the room to collect the next box, a smaller one, from the lobby. It was almost as heavy as the other crate.

"Imagine if this one had some treasure in it," Sam played. To his surprise she chuckled with him. "Let's see then? You open it."

He looked at her with great uncertainty, but the temptation was too much to bear. They put the box down. It made no sound to indicate that there was something inside, but the weight had their attention. The big ginger cat strolled into the room, following Sam.

"Hurry, the boss is hungry too," he winked.

Slowly Sam opened the lid, waiting for Nina to scare him with something sudden and loud. But it was Bruich that had them both thinking twice. The large cat stopped dead in his tracks and stared at the smaller box. Arching his back, his long hair stood on end all over his body, erect along his spine as he hissed at the box.

"Okay, I don't like that," Nina said solemnly. "Don't open it, Sam."

"I know this is a dumb thing to say, but Bruich's reaction has only made me curious now," Sam said. He watched the cat, calling him, but the cat would not move an inch closer to Sam. Instead, he turned around and ran out of the room.

"Bruich!" Nina called, chasing after the spooked feline.

Sam was amazed at the cat's behavior, but in his opinion the entire house was creepy. He hardly thought it was the box that upset Bruich. "Probably saw a bloody vampire in the closet," Sam sniggered to amuse himself and the silent room beckoned for him to open the lid.

Nina had caught up with Bruich in the living room. "Come on, sweety," she coaxed, picking up the cat and stroking him until he calmed down. "Don't be like Sam. There is nothing wrong with my house. Come, I have some treats for you in the kitchen."

She emptied out some juicy canned sardines for Bruich when she heard Sam calling from the other room. He sounded intrigued, and just a little uneasy.

"Nina!"

"Aye! What did you find?" she smiled.

"I don't know what this is about, but I think we should call Purdue!"

END

Made in the USA
San Bernardino, CA
11 July 2020